LAURA KOERBER

Encounters With Old Coyote

1

Chapter One: Old Coyote and the Professor

After Andrea died, she found herself in the condition of being a ghost. This was a surprise to her because, as an atheist, she'd assumed that death was the end. Oblivion. The absence of experience. No awareness or capacity for awareness. Her life as wife, novelist, and white middle class college professor hadn't prepared her for an afterlife, and yet there she was, a wisp of a gleam in the night air, floating over her dead body. She felt cheated and angry because it had taken quite a bit of determination on her part to die. It was an unpleasant shock to go through all that effort—a trip to Nevada, a bottle of wine, a handful of pills, plus a plastic bag over her head—just to find herself not quite altogether dead after all.

Andrea had traveled out to Basin and Range National Monument to die by starlight. Lymphoma, the doc said. He'd given her a few months to live. A widow with no children, Andrea had seen a nursing home in her future, and the prospect had depressed her more than death itself. So she'd made a plan to die outside where she could see the stars.

However, Iowa, her home state, wasn't a good place for laying around out of doors after dark. Too many mosquitoes, for one thing. A ritual of death interrupted repeatedly by bugs was too slapstick for Andrea's tastes. She hadn't wanted a lot of drama, and had hoped to get through the experience without crying, but slapping bugs? Not the right atmosphere for her last act.

The Monument wasn't totally bug-free, but there weren't any mosquitoes there. And the stars were stupendous, everything she'd hoped for, awesome beyond her capacity for words. In addition to the stars, vast periods of time were visible in the Great Basin as manifested in the petroglyphs on the rocks and, of course, the rocks themselves. In fact, the park included miles and miles of raw, wind-scoured, and water-ravaged geographical monuments to the passage of time. Andrea had wanted to die out where she could feel eternity and the Great Basin had met her need.

Except that she wasn't completely dead.

Andrea frowned at the black night air. What had gone wrong? She remembered everything clearly. She'd packed up and left Iowa only two days previously. Other than finding a home for her cat, she'd done very little to prep for her departure—just left a will on a scrap of paper giving her house and savings to the small publishing business that had published her six novels and her collection of short stories. With her will written and her cat re-homed, she'd walked out her front door, tossed a sleeping bag into her car, and abandoned her lifetime accumulation of stuff.

The abandonment of her belongings had been gut-wrenching. Her husband, Michael, had been a painter, and leaving the paintings behind had felt like an abandonment of Michael himself. But Michael had been dead for years. Gone. The hard fact, which Andrea had faced as resolutely as she'd faced the lymphoma, was that no one valued her lifetime accumulation of belongings. No one wanted any of it. All the stuff in her house—the paintings, the books, the knickknacks and keepsakes—all of that was going to end up in a landfill after her death.

Now, floating over her dead body while apparently still somewhat alive, her first thought was annoyance at her incomplete suicide, but her second thought was about her houseful of abandoned belongings. Maybe she should've killed herself back in Iowa so she could haunt her house? Maybe protect Michael's paintings which she'd left on the walls? "I'm sorry, Michael," she whispered. Then she was stabbed by a sudden thought. What if Michael was a ghost too? Was he haunting their home back in Iowa? Should she travel back to Iowa and look for him?

No. If he'd been haunting their house, he would've found a way to communicate with her. With that thought, a vast emptiness entered Andrea's heart. She was alone. The black night air wafted right through her. Her small fire had burned down to a golden spot like an earth-bound star, and her body lay curled up in the fetal position in her sleeping bag. She could see a gleam of reflected firelight on the plastic bag. She was all alone, a ghost in the darkness.

But wait a minute, she told herself, don't get all weepy and sad. The fact that *she* was a ghost meant that she couldn't be the only ghost in the world. There had to be others. Did animals have ghosts? Andrea lifted her eyes from her dead body and gazed out into the night. The distant mountains were visible only as the division between earth and starry sky. She could smell the thick, spicy scents of the desert but could see nothing of her surroundings but amorphous darkness. She could hear the rustle of leaves as a breeze stirred the sagebrush, but otherwise the desert was silent.

Was she even in Nevada anymore? Maybe she was in an alternative reality that looked like Nevada but wasn't. Andrea floated slowly in a circle as her eyes searched the darkness, but all she could see was the night air and the stars overhead. So many stars! Rampant stars spangling the sky from horizon to horizon. Stars with an infinity of space between them and beyond them. She'd expected to become part of that infinity, but instead she still existed, a wisp in the cool air of the night, aware and alone.

"God?" she asked. "Do you exist? Are you out there somewhere?" No one answered.

The next day Andrea saw the supernatural being. She'd spent most of the night curled up next to her body on the sleeping bag. Desolate and lost, what else could she do? Her body had looked frail and lonely, and she'd felt the same frailty and loneliness in what remained of her heart. In fact, she felt as if her ghost self was nothing more than her feelings expressed as a variation in the air. So, looking for comfort, she'd laid her ghost self down on the sleeping bag and curved herself around the small form of her body. All night long she'd studied the stars and worried about what the day would bring.

The dawn had arrived gently as the stars winked out and the sky shaded from black to gray to a tender blue. The mountains, lit by the morning sun, were briefly yellow, then blue, then settled into beige and dark green. Dusty and dry, the flat land around Andrea's campsite was a landscape of scrubby grass and sagebrush.

Andrea drifted slowly up and away from the body in the sleeping bag. She was feeling a lack of morning coffee and moved carefully, as if her ghost body might disintegrate, leaving her with nothing at all but a sad, disoriented consciousness. It was strange to get up and meet the day without any of the usual morning rituals: no breakfast, no teeth-brushing, no purring cat.

She looked around helplessly and was startled by the sight of her old car, parked on the edge of the dirt road. Solidly real, the hunk of metal and glass was in-congruent with the gentle, dream-like arrival of morning. Andrea hovered, confused, and stared at the car. It seemed to come from a different reality, a reality that had no room for a ghost. And yet there she was, a ghost in the air, just as real as the car, the sleeping bag, and the body.

Andrea hung in the air, thinking about the car, the road, and the long drive to the interstate. Should she leave? But why? Where would she go? On the other hand, should she stay? Bleakly, Andrea realized that days, maybe weeks and years, stretched ahead of her and she had no idea what to do with her existence.

She was rotating slowly in the air, looking around with growing desperation, when the spirit emerged from the dawn light. He came into being gently, as if created by the molecules of morning air: a shape not quite human, not quite coyote, and completely unlike anything she'd ever seen before. With a full head of spiky deer antlers, bluish gray fur, and yellow coyote eyes, he clearly was a supernatural manifestation.

Andrea stared into his yellow eyes, terrified. Her thoughts skittered around in her head. Should she fly away? Hide? But there was no place to hide in the flat, open landscape. She shrank back away warily and kept watch. The strange spirit approached her calmly, with the causal air of someone dropping in to visit a neighbor. Nodding briefly, he said, "Hi there."

Andrea made an effort to calm herself. After all, what could he do to her? She was already dead. Besides, she'd spent the night considering the possibility of a god, so maybe the sudden appearance of a spirit was providential. Had fate or death or God or a force of some sort sent her a source of answers? She put her fear aside and responded tentatively, "Hello?"

"I saw your fire," the spirit said.

Startled, Andrea realized that her small campfire still had some glowing black and orange embers. The spirit arranged himself on a rounded rock—a rock that Andrea hadn't noticed until he sat on it—and set out a coffee pot, a cup, and a canteen.

"Mind if I make some coffee?"

She had to clear her throat to get her voice working, "Go ahead."

"I can't make any for you," he commented. "Ghosts can't drink."

"Oh," Andrea said. She wafted into the airspace near the spirit and hovered awkwardly.

"So," the spirit said, "I can see your corpse over there."

Andrea winced at the word "corpse." She said, "Yes, I'm surprised to be a ghost. I didn't know ghosts were a real thing."

"There's lots of ghosts." He carefully prepared his coffee. His supplies, Andrea noticed, were kept in a painted parfleche like those she'd seen in a museum. The red, yellow, and black geometric design was from the Plains tribes. And he was wearing old style moccasins made with porcupine quills as decorations. His hands were brown and gnarly with long, knobby, twig-like fingers.

"What are you?" Andrea asked.

He gave her a brief glance before setting the pot on the coals.

"I'm what you humans call a spirit."

"You mean like a god? I mean like a local god, not the main one? If there is a main one." She felt embarrassed by her ignorance.

He grunted, a bit impatiently. "Those are all words. People make up words."

"Well, yeah." Tired of hovering, Andrea sank down on the sand. She folded her wispy body in on itself. "Just words," she said, "but that's what people do. We talk."

"Words." He shrugged.

If he's here to give me answers, she thought sourly, he's not doing a very good job. Andrea watched as the coyote poured himself a cup of coffee. She felt excluded by her inability to share the morning coffee ritual with him, but she didn't want him to leave either. She didn't want to be alone. At least not until she understood things better.

"Do animals have ghosts?" She was thinking of her old cat who would be dead soon.

He said, "I've seen some. Sometimes they wander around looking lost for a while."

"Lost?" Sorrow stabbed at Andrea. "I hope my cat just dies all the way. I don't want her to be hanging around..."

"Don't worry," he said. "It's mostly cows or horses. Or pigs. Some animal that had a really fucked up life. I don't think the happy ones become ghosts."

He doesn't think? Doesn't he know? Andrea studied the coyote out of the corner of her eyes. He was sipping the hot coffee with an air of contentment, maybe mixed with a little impatience. Impatience toward her?

Frustration seized Andrea. "I don't understand why I'm a ghost. I don't understand if there is a god or not. Is there a god?"

The coyote just looked at her and didn't answer. Stubbornly, Andrea forged ahead, "Because I never believed in one but here I am, a ghost sitting with a supernatural being." She paused, but Coyote was involved in carefully picking his long yellow teeth. Andrea plunged on, "The reason I never believed in God is because of people acting like he was their personal on-demand life coach or sugar daddy. My ex sister-in-law, I mean the sister of my first husband, was like that. One time we were over to her house for dinner just before Christmas. She was real religious in a Bible-quoting kind of way. Anyway, she was all excited because she'd found a Cabbage Patch Doll for her daughter." She glanced at Coyote and saw that she'd finally caught his interest. He had one eyebrow cocked. "She said she'd been running all over town trying to find one, but they were the big fad that year and every store was bought out. Then she decided to pray and, after praying, she tried one last store. And, in that one last store, there was one last Cabbage Patch Doll. She told us that Jesus himself had intervened to get that gift for her daughter." Andrea didn't try to keep the sneer out of her voice. "So I asked her. I asked if Jesus got a doll for your daughter, why didn't he save six million Jews?"

Coyote grinned.

"Because they weren't Christians. That's what she said."

"Yup. That's humans for you." He set his cup down.

"So," she said, "just to be clear, is there a god that answers prayers? Or not?"

"I don't think so."

Andrea burst out. "Don't you know? You're a spirit. You know about this stuff. What do you mean you just don't think so?"

"I mean," he said calmly, "that I don't think so. I've seen prayers get answered and prayers not get answered. Either there's a god that's arbitrary, or there's a god that doesn't care, or maybe there isn't a god and sometimes people just get lucky. Personally, I'd sooner bet on a poker hand than bet on a prayer."

Andrea had to laugh even though she was pretty pissed off. "But," she sputtered, "aren't you a god of sorts? Kind of?"

Coyote set his coffee cup down on the dirt beside his rock. He settled himself as if getting ready to stay awhile and said, "Not the way you mean it." He glanced at Andrea, grimaced, and said, "Okay, I'll try to explain. Since you humans like stories, I'll try to explain that way. I'll tell you some stories."

2

Chapter Two: Coyote Tells a Story

"I'm what the anthropologists call a trickster." His shoulders lifted briefly in an ironic shrug. "They say I represent the forces of chaos and change. Or chaos and creativity." He fumbled in his coat pocket—Andrea realized for the first time that he was wearing dark blue frock coat—and extricated a beat up pack of cigarettes. "And maybe I am." He snapped a small flame into existence with his knobby fingers. "But mostly I'm just me. Like the rocks are rocks. Or plants are plants." He took a deep drag on the cigarette and added, "But here's a story. When I was young a long, long, long time ago and new to the world, I used to talk to humans all the time."

"Wait, what?" Andrea interrupted. "You were new to the world?"

"Yeah, I think I showed up about the time humans got enough brains to imagine things. About the time they started painting on rocks. Anyway, you want to hear this story or not?"

"I do," said Andrea. She hunched her shoulders. "Sorry." But she didn't feel apologetic. For most of her life she'd been comfortable with ambiguity, but now that her existence itself was ambiguous, she wanted clear answers. Still, Coyote was better than no one, and she didn't want to be alone. She settled in to listen.

With a side-eye glance at her, Coyote, relaunched his story, "I thought humans were pathetic. Always chattering and arguing and gossiping. They used to tell all kinds of stories about me, and sometimes the stories were about me giving them fire or taking fire away from them and so on. Different people told different stories. That's one thing about people—they need to tell stories. They can't stop themselves. Stories all the time. That's how they understand things.

"Well, anyway I was just minding my own business when some humans came along and saw me." He stopped talking so he could pick his teeth again. Then he resumed, "They knew I wasn't like them." Coyote shrugged. "Since I wasn't like them, they jumped to conclusions, I guess, and started asking me about stuff they didn't understand. One of the things they asked me was why the moon disappeared and came back again over and over. Well, I knew why; it had to do with the earth and the sun and the rotations. You probably learned all that in school, right?"

"Yeah. I'm not sure I could explain it, but yeah."

"I could've explained it, but what fun would there be in that? So I told them that I ate the moon. I said I nibbled on it a little everyday until it was just about gone, and then I stopped and let it grow back. Since I never ate it all up, it always came back and then there was more for me for later."

He grinned, and his eyes gleamed with cynicism. "Well, they sure liked that story. They told each other how wise I was and how they could apply the principle of sustainability to their hunting and gathering techniques. 'Always leave a little,' they told their kids. 'Coyote understands this stuff so take a lesson from him.'" Coyote grinned, showing a lot of teeth. He inhaled on his cigarette and ashed on the ground.

"So..." Andrea asked, "what are you saying? That you aren't... aren't really...I don't get it."

He shrugged. "I told them stories, and they...they added stuff onto the story, stuff that was good for them. They made the stories into more than just me fucking with them. Like I said, that's how people understand things. By telling stories. Besides, back before TV and books and the Internet, what else was there to do? People were epic story tellers back in the day. Some of their stories took a week to tell and got recited from memory. Here's another story.

"This is how humans learned to use spears. I was out and about one fine day, not doing anything in particular, when I met up with Rabbit. Rabbit was a smart ass. Always making a big deal out of himself. Always one for the ladies, showing off, and always one for getting into fights. Did you know that rabbits got into pissing matches?"

"No."

"Well, they do. That's where that phrase comes from when someone says some guys are in a pissing match. Male rabbits will box like kangaroos, but they also shoot pee at each other. Anyway, here goes the story:

So there I was, minding my own business, and I ran into Rabbit who immediately started in on me. Said he could outrun me. Said he could out jump me. Even said he could out piss me. So I took up the challenge. I got a stick and drew a line in the dirt. Then we backed up a ways, and some bird up in a tree called out,

"Ready, set, go," and off we went. I made it to the line in five long bounds. But, while I was leaping, Rabbit was scampering and he really can move when he wants to. "Rabbit won!" the bird yelled. I don't remember what kind of bird it was since this all happened a long long time ago, but I bet it was a jay.

So Rabbit won. It wouldn't have pissed me off—there's that peeing theme again—except he bragged so damn much. And he said he could jump farther than me too.

So this time we used the line in the dirt as the starting place. I went first. I got myself all poised and wound up and ready, and then I sprang with all of my might. I made a lovely elegant leap and landed about fifteen feet away. The jay flew down and marked my landing spot with a small rock.

Then it was Rabbit's turn. He squatted down, hunched over, and then unleashed a spring that sent him sailing through the air. I guess because he was smaller than me, he was airborne longer. He landed about a foot past the rock that marked where I'd landed.

And, being an asshole, he had to brag about it.

That left pissing. I knew rabbits got into pissing contests, but I thought I'd be able to shoot more piss than a little bitty asshole like Rabbit.

Both of us headed to the creek and tanked up. Then we went back and I drew another line with my stick. We toed the line and held it until Jay said "GO!"

My pee went in an arc out across the line and down into the dirt. I peed for a long time. But that little shit, that Rabbit. He didn't pee for long, but what he had he shot clear out five or six feet. He was low on ammo but could shoot long distance.

Jay said Rabbit had won again. Rabbit got all smug about it and said, "Is there any kind of contest you *can* win, Coyote?

Anything at all? Or are you just a loser?"

So I grabbed up the stick and said, "I can stab you faster than you can get away."

He was fast, I'll say that for him, but not fast enough. I threw that stick *hard* and I skewered the little bastard. Jay yelled, "You killed him!" and I said, "I can eat him faster than he can get away, too."

Jay then flew away and went around telling everyone how I'd killed Rabbit with a stick. That got the humans talking and pretty soon they were killing animals by using spears.

In fact, some scientists claim that they, the humans, were the cause of the megafauna of the Pleistocene dying out. The story is that when humans crossed the bridge to this continent, they were top predators and over-hunted all the horses and giant sloths and so on. That's one story, anyway.

Finished, Coyote lounged back against his rock.

"Did they?"Andrea asked.

He shrugged and said, "I don't think so. I think it was climate change that did them in. It was one of those Ice Age climate changes. See? More evidence that there isn't anyone in charge because why fuck up creation? It's not like those giant sloths and woolly mammoths deserved to die."

"Okay." Andrea frowned in an effort to understand. "So you've been around since the Pleistocene, but you don't know for sure if there is a god or not...because you don't see any signs of one? But humans have treated you kind of like a god? Because you're a catalyst? You get them thinking?"

"My point is you worrying about whether or not there's a god in charge is a human thing to do. All religions are stories. All of them have bits that are probably true, in my opinion, but mostly they're junked up with a lot of extra baggage about...this ritual or that dogma and so on. Stories." He sat back, set his cup down and said, "Now it's your turn. You tell a story."

"Hmm," Andrea murmured. Coyote had got her thinking about her own spirituality, such as it was. She rummaged around in her mind. "Well, I guess I have a story." She glanced up. Coyote's oddly human face was smiling, but not friendly or unfriendly. Distant, like he was more interested in his coffee than her. She felt intimidated. What story could she tell that would be entertaining to this ancient spirit? "I lost my bra at a truck stop near the Arctic Circle."

"Good beginning." He grinned. "Let's hear it."

"That's most of the story right there." But she'd started so she kept going. "I wanted to go to the Arctic Circle because I wanted to see a real wilderness. This was back in the nineties, pre-climate change. I wouldn't go up there now."

Coyote shrugged. "Nothing on earth is eternal."

"But it's different when life is fucked up by careless, selfish, and irresponsible people who know what they're doing," Andrea said with heat. "Humans didn't *have* to destroy everything. Man-made climate change is *not* the same thing as mass extinctions through random acts of geology triggering major changes in the ecology."

He shrugged again.

Andrea nearly ground her teeth with annoyance, but she didn't seem to have teeth. A nature spirit, she thought, should be angry about the willful destruction of nature by humans. Instead he seemed to think that all the death and suffering was just... another episode in a very long existence—even when the death and the suffering were unnecessary.

Well, she couldn't change how he felt, so she started her

story again. "I flew up to Whitehorse, Yukon Territory, and hopped into a car. It was a Mercury Mustique, and it leaked dust something awful. Anyway, from there I drove north to the gravel highway that goes almost to the Arctic ocean.

"It's a highway for oil tanker trucks, so there's that climate change theme again. And, yes, I knew I was part of it because I was driving one of the cars that killed the world. But what else could I do? I knew about climate change. I'd known about it since the seventies, but no one seemed to care, and there was nothing going on at all to prevent the catastrophe. So I went up to see the wilderness before it was destroyed, and I knew I was part of the destruction."

"There's some poet guy who said something about men always destroy what they love," said Coyote.

Andrea snorted derisively. "Oscar Wilde had a gift for being glibly superficial. He was talking about people destroying people they love. But it is true that Americans destroyed the land we supposedly loved."

"Back to the story," said Coyote.

He had caused the digression! "Back to the story," Andrea said, irritated. "I drove up that road..."

3

Chapter Three: How I Lost My Bra at a Truck Stop in Yukon Territory

She let herself slide into memory. A picture formed in her mind of a valley brilliant with violet fireweed, so vibrant under the arctic sun that she had to squint. Dark green fir trees huddled along the base of the mountains. The gray rocky slopes rose abruptly, slanting upwards to jagged peaks that snagged the bellies of the passing clouds. The height of the mountains was an illusion. In fact, they weren't really mountains at all—just huge, steep-sided hills—but they looked like mountains because the valley floor was the treeline. A twenty foot elevation rise was enough to cause a change in the plant life from forest to treeless rocks covered by lichen, moss, and strange arctic plants she couldn't name. "I remember," Andrea said, "how beautiful it was."

I was there in August, and the fireweed in the valley of the Klondike River was in full glory while the strange arctic plants on the mountain sides were turning every shade of copper, gold, and russet against the background of blue-gray rocks. It was a stark landscape, a landscape where the cold of winter could be felt even in the warmth of the sun. The trees were much older than they appeared to be. Stunted by decades of short summers and limited growth opportunities, they were veterans of innumerable winters. The rocky peaks and crags thrusting upwards above the treeline made a statement in raw geology about time, reminding me of how old the earth was and how briefly I would live.

I drove north. As I drove, I stared off into the landscape, looking, looking, looking until I had eye strain. I saw beauty in everything: the curve of the road through a meadow, clouds reflected in a lake, the intricate matrix of muskeg and spruce along the road, the vibrant colors of the wildflowers. I stopped at a river, got out of my car, and walked down to the water's edge. The river was wild in a way rarely possible in the lower forty-eight. Lined with lush green rushes, the water was clear and clean and slid easily over golden brown rocks. A dragonfly glittered in the air. I watched a pair of wild swans ride the current downstream. Suddenly time stopped and all thought left my mind. I felt completely at peace.

Later, when I came back to myself, I headed north again. From a ridge, I stopped to take in a view across the valley of the Mackenzie River to distant mountains that were white, but not with snow. Miles of white rock mountains reflected light against the ultramarine of the cloudy sky. The valley itself was a study in textures from the woolly green willows to the thickly green water meadows. It was an impossible landscape, too wet for man or beast to travel but beautiful beyond all imagination. I kept driving north, one eyeball organism after another, through the cold, raw Eden.

But no one can stay in a state of awe for long. A couple hours and I don't now how many kilometers later, I found myself rolling along a narrow gravel road that crossed a wide green plain. The wind was blowing hard enough to shake my car, so I didn't get out to look at the flowers—but flowers were everywhere. Yellow bursts of color, fluffy white puffs, tiny blue flowers so fragile they formed a haze. I rounded a corner and saw a big sign with a parking lot. I pulled in because I had arrived. The Arctic Circle.

Rain spattered across my windshield. I'd been in the car all day, staring out the windows and searching the landscape for that ultimate beauty. My brain was full of images of plants and rocks and water. I was mentally exhausted. Then a double rainbow appeared. It arched from horizon to horizon, full spectrum, spectacular. I thought, "The Goddess of Vacations has just given me a prize!" and I felt deeply grateful for everything I had seen that day.

Tired and sore from being seated too long, I turned around and drove south to Eagle Plain where there was a truck stop, a motel, and an unpleasant campground. I put up my tent on the edge of the campground with the door facing north toward a darkening sky. Then I gathered up a change of clothing and my shower stuff and crossed the muddy parking lot to the motel. There was a shower building for campers, but I needed to go by the front desk of the motel to trade my paper money for the dollar coins Canadians call "loonies". Mission accomplished, I left the motel and entered the shower building. The shower was pleasant, especially after all the stiffness of driving. Finished, I dried off and started getting dressed in my clean clothes.

But I couldn't find my bra. Maybe I'd left it in the tent? Braless but otherwise dressed, I headed back across the windy, cold parking lot and peered into the tent. No bra. I fumbled though my duffle bag. No bra.

With a sinking feeling, I mentally retraced my route...and oops. So I dumped my toothbrush and my dirty clothes in the tent and set out once again across the parking lot to the motel. The lobby had two big glass doors with a good view of the front desk where I had exchanged my Canadian dollars for loonies. Along one side of the lobby, five or six truck drivers were seated. In the middle of the floor was my bra.

It wasn't a pretty bra. Just basic JC Penny's. It looked utterly pathetic all alone in the middle of the lobby. I slowly backed away from the glass doors. Then I did a pivot and made a beeline for my tent.

The next morning I woke up hungry, but I didn't go the motel restaurant to eat. I was afraid someone would get all helpful and say, "Here's the bra you dropped." I didn't get a chance to buy an Arctic Circle commemorative T-shirt from their souvenir shop either."

Andrea checked Coyote's face for his reaction.

"Heh, heh," Coyote sniggered. "I coulda rescued it for you."

"That's not the point," Andrea said. She waited for him to make some comment about the beauty of the wilderness or her love for the beauty, but Coyote just helped himself to another cup of coffee. He didn't seem to have anything to say about her...well, 'worship' wasn't quite the right word for her attitude toward nature. Respect? Her belief that humans should have more respect for the forces of creation and for what those forces had created. Her belief that humans were part of, not above, that creation. But Coyote was just sitting there, smoking and sipping his coffee, with nothing to say except juvenile giggling about her bra.

"I have another story about spirituality. Wanna hear it?" She didn't say that second story had come to her mind because of how disappointed she was in Coyote.

He leaned back on his rock and blew a smoke ring. "Sure."

Nettled, she started her story.

4

Chapter Four: Putting the Shard Back

"I was hiking in a canyon in southern Utah with my brother on a really hot day," Andrea paused, remembering, "and I said to him, 'This would be a good place to die, but not today.'" Her eyes slid toward her sleeping bag and the slight form curled up within. "This happened back when I was still alive, when I was about seventy and thinking about places to die. Thinking about things I owned and what would happen to those things without me."

She hesitated because her mind was full of memory, then began the story in earnest:

The heat was getting to me. My knees felt soft and mushy, and my head was beginning to float. The canyon had trapped hot air. Probably up at the top of the orange rock walls there was a cool breeze, but down in the hot sand, on the trail between the gnarly live oaks and the thick water rushes, the air was packed with heat. I was on a pilgrimage to my personal holy land, a place called Calf Creek Canyon in Escalante/Staircase National Monument, with the intention of returning an ancient pottery shard to the people who had once lived there. I'd picked the canyon out as a good place to die, but this all happened back when I was still basically healthy and death was still an abstraction to me.

So there I was, hiking up the canyon on my pilgrimage with the shard in my pocket, and it was so hot in the canyon that my body was rebelling, telling me to get out of the sun and sit down.

My brother stopped. ''Too hot for you?'' he asked. His bald head was protected by a bandanna, but his face was reddening. We dug out our water bottles and slurped up the elixir of life.

"Yeah, I think it's too hot. I just don't have the stamina I used to have." We were on a six mile in-and-out hike that I'd done before. The first time was back in the seventies. A friend and I drove over the mountain—this is back before the road was paved—and stumbled onto the canyon completely by accident. We were stoned, of course. We'd been driving around smoking pot for days, just absorbing the fierce beauty of the West. At Calf Creek we stopped, stunned into a state of awe.

That whole area of southern Utah is carved into a landscape of canyons, nothing but naked geology for miles. Huge humps of white rock were scoured by the wind into rounded shapes like earth-bound clouds. Below the white rocks, the canyonlands are orange and carved by water into a fascinating wonderland of ravines, drainages, and canyons where every corner entices exploration.

On that first hike back in the seventies, my friend and I hiked all the way to the ridiculously photogenic waterfall at the end of the trail. There we revived ourselves by sticking our feet in the water. It was so cold that the shock ran right up our legs and spread throughout our bodies. We looked up at the top of the waterfall and wondered what the canyon was like up there.

On the way back, we saw the horned gods painted on the canyon wall. They were still there after thousands of years, staring stoically out at tourists like us from at the base of the canyon on the far side of the creek. More on them later, Coyote.

We went back to the truck, dug out our sleeping bags and the very minimum of supplies, and set out to explore. I'm amazed now at what we did. We climbed up out of the canyon. We just picked a place and said, "Let's try here." The canyon walls are about as high as a six or seven story building. The place we picked wasn't sheer, but very steep. However, the canyon wall was broken with deep gouges and cracks and crumbled places. Here and there scrappy little trees grew out of the rocks. We clambered and scrambled. At one point I wrapped my arms around a tree and my friend climbed up my body. Once on the ledge above, he pulled me up. We made it to the top and saw a world of canyons to the east and west and south. Mountains were to the north.

We walked along on top, and it was like walking on clouds made of stone. We found water in pools on the rock. We found a lovely pink arrowhead. We slept under the stars. The next day we made the much easier and much shorter descent down into the canyon above the falls. That stretch of canyon was thick with trees and moist humid air, with nearly impenetrable underbrush. We saw cougar prints and decided to leave.

That was the first time I made the hike. Since then I've hiked the canyon six or seven more times, each time with an older body and less resilience to heat.

So that summer, the summer I hiked the canyon with my brother, I was carrying a pottery shard in my pocket. It was a small fragment of a handmade container that had once held water, probably. Thin and dry, it was textured on one side and smooth on the other. No color except the dark beige of the clay itself. Someone's fingers had shaped it hundreds of years ago.

I picked it up at Hovenweep over on the Colorado border when I was twelve or so from what used to be called an Anasazi site, but now is referred to as Ancient Pueblo Culture. A few ruined pueblo-style homes remain there in a chaotic landscape of canyons, ravines, ridges, hills, and mesas. Mostly the ruins had been raided by pot hunters years ago. My family was camping there, and the ancient ruins weren't protected from random white people and their kids.

Somehow I'd hung on to that pottery shard for decades. That shard followed me to college and made the move from Iowa to Seattle. It then traveled to back to Iowa and ended up in our house, the home I shared with Michael. But, as I got older, I'd started worrying about the demise of all of my stuff. Upon my death, would the shard end up in a landfill? Dumped with other remnants of my life? I didn't expect the things I made or the things I cherished to live forever, but I didn't want to be the cause of the demise of the ancient pottery shard.

So one of my reasons for going back to Calf Creek Canyon was to return the shard. I wasn't returning it to its home at Hovenweep, but Calf Creek was close enough culturally and physically. After all, there's plenty of evidence that the people of the southwest had all kinds of interactions with each other including trade. The people who worshiped the horned gods had used pottery like my shard, so I had it wrapped up in cloth and stashed in my pocket to be returned. I wanted to leave the shard for the gods of the people of the canyon.

I knew the gods were in the canyon somewhere just above a pile of rocky debris. They'd been painted on one of the places where nearly the whole canyon wall was smooth and a dark purplish red. All morning as we hiked, I'd been searching the canyon wall, looking for the ancient paintings of the gods.

But my vision had started getting blurry, so I knew I had to stop. We found a handy fallen log shaded by some twisted old oaks where I could sit. I sank down gratefully into the blessing of shadow and drank more water while my brother headed up the trail.

Disappointment set in. I'd really wanted to lay the shard down somewhere near the gods, not just at some random place in the canyon. They weren't my gods, obviously. And I didn't know what they'd meant to the people who'd worshiped them. They could've represented evil for all I knew, though I thought it was more likely that they represented the natural forces that had sustained their lives.

I'm not naive about the people who painted the gods. I don't think they were Noble Savages. They were humans and given to the failings of all people. The archaeological record shows warfare. Also murder and possibly torture. They'd stashed their seed corn in granaries up high in the canyon walls, possibly out of fear that raiders would steal their supply. It's also possible that they were just keeping their seed corn away from mice. Either way, I think it is likely that they, like all humans, were essentially wolves: territorial, hierarchical pack hunters who preyed on other people and were preyed on by them.

However, they didn't destroy the world around them as we have done. Maybe they would've if they could've. They were hunters, gatherers, and small scale farmers, so there was a limit to how much harm they could do to their world. On the other hand, if the contemporary Pueblo cultures are anything to go by, they were deeply respectful of and grateful to the natural world and didn't engage in careless destruction from short term thinking and acquisitiveness.

I admire the ancient culture—that is, I admire what I think they believed about their role in the natural world. So, sitting there in the canyon and thinking about how our contemporary culture was causing global catastrophe, I wondered if the gods were gone. Maybe I wouldn't be able to find them. Maybe they had abandoned the canyon. Or maybe they were still present but not showing themselves to me. As I sat, I kept on searching the canyon with my eyes, hoping that I would find them.

The canyon wall across from my shady refuge looked right. The cliff was flat, red, and tall. There was a debris pile at the base. There was also a long slanting shadow from the canyon top down to the rocky debris. The sun-struck face of the cliff was golden red, while the shadowed area was nearly purple with darkness. I watched the canyon wall for what seemed like a long time.

As time passed, the shadow moved, revealing more of the canyon wall. And then, suddenly, I saw them. The three stylized figures were still there, standing side by side and staring out at the canyon as they had for a thousand years. Their eyes held the implacable gaze of superior beings who had been in the canyon forever and had no intention of going away. There's nothing you can do to us, they were saying. We are still here. We always will be here until this planet falls into the sun. We are as long-lived as the rocks. We might weather away, but as long as there is an earth, we will be here.

I was so grateful so see them, Coyote. I felt lucky and thankful.

"Okay," I said to the gods. "I have something for you." I found a crack in a rock on my side of the canyon, across Calf Creek from the gods. I tucked the shard deep into the crack where it would be safe for ... who knows? Maybe another thousand years.

5

Chapter Five: A Small Town in Arkansas

"Huh. I liked your bra story better."

Andrea shot him a look of annoyance. "I have a question. Are the horned gods real? I mean, real like you are? Spirits of some kind?"

Coyote shrugged. "People probably acted the way they thought the gods wanted them to act. That's a kind of reality."

"So what the gods represented was real? But maybe not the actual gods?"

"Close enough." Coyote shifted position and squinted at the sky. The cool of nighttime was gone, and the heat of day was seeping in as the sun rose above the distant mountains. Coyote stretched, yawned, and otherwise gave indications of not being sufficiently amused by Andrea's company. She could see hours ahead with the two of them sitting in awkward silence. Awkward on her part, at least. And there was nothing to stop Coyote from just getting up to leave. The thought of being alone filled her with sadness.

"I could tell you some more stories," she offered. "Nothing

serious. Just stuff that happened."

"Sure." He sat back, making himself comfortable. I guess he doesn't have anything else to do right now, Andrea thought. Which brought a question to her mind: What did he do with his time? But she saved the question for later and started on some reminiscences. "This story is about a camping trip I went on with my family. We were always off camping somewhere. I guess that's where I got my love of nature. But this story is about a strange little town in Arkansas."

My father emerged from the bar cradling a six pack. His expression was bemused. He crossed the gravel parking lot, opened the driver's side door, and dropped onto the driver's seat. The beer landed on my mother's lap.

"Coors?" she asked, eyebrows raised.

Dad stuck the key in the ignition. He paused, then said, "Well."

We were deep in the wooded hills of Arkansas on our way to Texas about a week before Christmas on a family camping trip aimed at the Gulf Coast. Our destination for the night was a state park campground near a spot on the map called Tom Horton. Not exactly a town, the spot consisted of a low-slung shabby tavern—windowless and covered with fading ads for motor oil and beer—a cottage or two, and a gas station. Since the spot on the map lacked a grocery, my dad had gone into the tavern to buy beer.

Still looking bemused, he told my mom, "I asked the bartender if she'd sell me a six pack and she said yes. Then she asked me what kind of beer I wanted, so I said the cheapest. Then she said they were all the same price, so I asked for Bud. Then she said they only had one brand, Coors." He turned the key and started the car. "So that's why I got Coors."

My mom lit a cigarette. This was back in the sixties when both of my parents smoked. We drove hundreds of miles every vacation with no seat belts, and my parents drank beer while driving. In fact, one time my mom's cigarette set her skirt on fire and my dad put the fire out by pouring beer on it—all without stopping the car. My dad was a college professor and had summers off which we spent camping all over the West. Over Christmas, we headed south.

They both cracked their beers open and made faces while they sipped. I don't know why people who drank Bud would object to Coors—but I don't drink beer at all, so what do I know? I think the objection was more political than anything else or maybe the beer wasn't cheap enough for their standards. I was just a kid and along for the ride.

We got into the campground around dinner time. To enter the campground, we crossed a ford in a small river. The cement gleamed with green moss and was slippery, just on the edge of frozen. The campground was empty of people but thick with trees, mostly leafless against the gray sky. My folks chose a site that overlooked the lake. Us kids spilled out and milled around, chilly and hungry. Mom started unpacking the kitchen stuff and Dad went for water.

He stopped at the edge of our site and pointed at a branch that extended over the campground road. "Look at that."

Mom glanced up. "Someone had a bad day." A fishing fly was dangling from the branch.

"Picked a bad place to practice his cast," Dad said. He set off on his mission to get water. Mom saw us kids standing there looking useless, so she put us to work gathering firewood.

After Dad came back with the water, he picked a site for our tent. I helped put it up. It was a huge saggy affair made of canvas stained with mold and worn from use. I was putting tension on a tent pole while Dad pounded in a tent peg when I saw the teenager. Being twelve myself, the teenager—who looked to be about sixteen—was innately cool just by virtue of being older than me. He was slouching slowly around the circle of the campground. Every now and then he shot a glance at us.

"I wonder who he belongs to?" my mom commented. Then she called us to dinner.

Generally speaking, my mom was a lousy cook, but she excelled when it came to processing a meal over a fire or a Coleman stove. Or maybe it was the cold air and the exercise that made her Spanish rice palatable. We dived in, stuffing our faces. Meanwhile the kid found a picnic table to sit on. There he slumped, barely visible though the brush, his back to the lake. Immobile. Not smoking. Not drinking. Just sitting. He was a skinny kid, and his jacket was too thin for the cold evening.

The sound of a truck splashing through the ford spooked the kid. He jumped off the table and disappeared. A pick up truck rolled into view and stopped short of the fishing fly, still dangling from the tree branch. A large angry man emerged from the truck, holding a shotgun. We all stopped eating.

The man aimed the shotgun at the fly and blasted away. The shots scared a murder of crows up into the gray sky but did nothing to the dangling fly. He reloaded and fired again. This time the branch took a hit, splintered, but hung on by a few shreds of bark. The fly swung back and forth out of reach. The angry man loaded up again, took a few strides closer, and blasted away. The branch surrendered and landed with a thump on the road.

The man tossed the gun into his truck and stomped over to the fly. He snatched it up. Since the fly was still tied to the tangled fishing line, the branch came up too. The branch was about the size of the man's arm. There was a brief fight between the man, the fishing line, and the branch before the man, steaming with exasperation, carried the whole mess back to the truck, tossed everything in, and left.

"That was entertaining," said my dad.

The teenager emerged from the brush and climbed up on the picnic table.

"Do you think we should offer him some food?" my dad asked. My mother, who thought the three kids she had were three too many, said no.

"He's in some kind of trouble, and it will get sorted out by someone," she predicted. Sure enough, while us three kids were doing the dishes, we heard another splash. This time it was a police car.

It was getting dark but the kid was still visible as a profile against the lake, still perched on the picnic table. The cop drove around, stopped, and got out of his vehicle. He was a heavy man with a ponderous walk. The kid watched him approach and made no effort to flee.

I was enough of an adolescent that I wanted the kid to be heroically defiant and rebellious, but he wasn't. After a few minutes of conversation, the kid got in the squad car and they drove away.

"Well, I'm glad he's not out here freezing," said my dad. Night had fallen and with it the last remains of warmth. Chilly had become just plain cold. We sat around a fire for a while, then turned in. Snuggled into our sleeping bags, we played geography to put ourselves to sleep. The letter was T.

"Tennessee," I said

"Texas," said my sister.

"Titania," said my mother. "It's one of the moons for Uranus."

"That doesn't count," we all protested.

"Why not? No one said the geography had to be on earth," my mother argued. We let her have it.

"Trubchevsk," said my dad, who was infamous for cheating by making up Russian-sounding place names. After a brief argument, it was my brother's turn.

"Thailand," he said, and the night was assaulted by shots from multiple guns. An engine revved and roared in the dark. Voices shouted drunken nonsense. My mother threw her body over me, and my dad rolled over my sister. More gunshots. Mom grabbed at my brother's sleeping bad to pull him closer. "Stay down," she whispered.

The truck growled, taking the corners too fast. Gravel shot like shrapnel at our campsite. There was incomprehensible drunken hollering in voices both male and female. Glass exploded against the ground—they must've thrown a wine bottle at us. Night Train or Boone's Farm, no doubt. The truck roared off. More shots, probably a deer rifle. We heard the splashing when the truck hit the ford. Tires screamed and an abrupt silence told the story.

We lay in the silence, listening intently.

My sister whispered, "What are they doing now?"

"Hush," said my mom.

A crunch of gravel indicated footsteps. We lay rigid and silent. A quiet female voice asked, "Hello?" A childish voice said, "They're asleep," and a third voice, male, said, "Wake them up."

Oddly, the drunken assholes sounded like a family. We didn't move a muscle or make a sound.

The people on the road dithered and whispered. Evidently the crash had sobered them up. Then, to our relief, we heard the gravel crunching as they moved away. We lay listening for a long time. I pictured the drunken locals, now somewhat sober, trudging wearily down the gravel road toward the highway. This all happened back before cell phones.

Finally my mother rolled away. My dad spoke in the darkness, "If we were good Samaritans, we would've helped them."

"Good thing we aren't, then," said my mom. Then she asked, "Whose turn is it?"

"Mine," I said. With an effort, I dredged up a name. "Tom Horton."

"What's that?" my sister demanded.

"It's the name of that weird little town where everyone drinks Coors. The town we came through to get here."

"Okay." We went on with our game until everyone got too sleepy to think of place names.

I'm boring him, Andrea though. Coyote had nodded off and was gently snoring. Andrea wondered what she would do if Coyote decided to leave. Would she trail after him, lonely and desperate? Would she hang around her corpse? A wave of desperation washed through her. She *couldn't* just hang there in the air, hovering over a dead body, lost and confused. If Coyote left, she would follow. Meanwhile, she'd tell him stories, whether he was listening or not.

"Can dreams come true, Coyote?" His head was bent down, his chin on his chest, his eyes buried in furry wrinkles. "Can dreams *be* true?"

She waited. One of his ears flicked a fly away. "I had a dream about you once. It was the scariest dream of my life because it felt absolutely real." The fly resettled on the tip of his ear. A silence lengthened. "Are you dreaming?" Andrea asked. Then she sighed and started the story.

"I'm not sure if this story is about me or someone else. I woke up a couple mornings ago while I was still alive with this story in my head, as intense as a real experience. It's a story about a strange vacation involving heroic cows, a mysterious coyote man, and a dog." Andrea glanced at Coyote to see how he'd react, but he was still asleep.

"After I woke up, I retold the story to myself a couple of times to get it stuck in my short term memory. Then I went down stairs, got some coffee, and typed the whole thing out. Not creative writing. Just a bashed-out narrative rampant with typos. I titled it, "The Dream." Then I hit "save as" and it vanished."

Coyote shifted his position and settled his back against against a rock. He tipped his black cowboy hat over his eyes.

Andrea frowned. Where had the hat come from and how was he wearing it over his antlers? Weird. "Gone," she said, insistent that he notice her story. "It really was strange. The computer just swallowed it. Or it got sucked up somewhere, retracted by whatever force gave me the story in the first place." Andrea laughed shortly. "That was a scary thought! Like some force didn't want me to remember the dream. But probably I'd just screwed myself as usual with incompetence. Technophobia strikes again! So I typed the damn thing over again, this time really rushing, just bish, bash, bish, bash. I could feel the intensity of the story fading from my mind as I typed, but nevertheless, I got the whole thing down.

"I hit save and it vanished again. It really was creepy." She stopped. Coyote was awake, sort of, and smoking again. "I had this feeling that something was watching me. Scary." She shuddered, then laughed again. "I didn't believe in ghosts or anything back when this happened, so...maybe something really was watching me and erasing the story?" Coyote grunted noncommittally. "I hunted and hunted for it. Documents, downloads, the trashcan, those recondite places my computer sends stuff every now and then...My story had just disappeared. Twice.

"So I got kind of freaked out. But I typed the whole thing out again. I'm not going to tell it in first person because I didn't dream it that way. Here goes:"

6

Chapter Six: A Dream of Cows and Creepy People

The vibrating was irritating and her butt was sore. She sat with her arms locked around her knees, shaking in time with the thrum of the engine, bored, but unable to relax. They'd been aloft for hours, winging across vast expanses of land, but she'd seen nothing but the harsh dirty yellow of the windowless cargo hold. In her boredom, she'd spent some time softly singing to herself with the engine providing back up music. Then she set her imagination loose on the rust spots, envisioning them as islands in the sea of yellow metal. She identified harbors and established trade routes. She even invented wind and weather patterns. Maybe her vacation was going to be a bust. It was a possibility.

She'd assumed that the plane would have windows. Wasn't that a natural assumption to make? She bought the plane ticket for just that reason: to sit by the window and watch all the geography roll by. The flight itself was supposed to be part of her vacation. She should've realized that there was something wrong with a ticket so cheap.

So instead of watching the earth from a seat in the sky, she was stuck staring at a curved metal wall from an uncomfortable spot on the floor. Still, she told herself, she was going somewhere she'd never been before and the novelty would be fun. Right? She was going out West to a small town that wasn't a tourist destination. It was a real place occupied by people who weren't catering to outsiders. A slightly scary place, judging by the ad. "On the Edge" was the slogan. "Edge" capitalized as if it was a place name.

The sound of the engine changed, grew louder and more concentrated. The plane shivered from front to back and roared. They hit the ground, bounced, and g-forces nearly knocked her over. Finally the noise lessened to a loud purr and the plane rolled to a stop. She unfolded her stiff body and stood up. Then she dragged her backpack to the open door of the cargo hold. There she decanted herself awkwardly on to the tarmac and wriggled her shoulders into her back pack. The pilot watched, not helpful, not interested.

It was unbelievably hot. They were out on a bleak stretch of asphalt in the midst of a bleaker expanse of yellow prairie. There was nothing to see but a row of shabby rusted Quonset huts. The pilot slammed the door of the cargo hold. The possibility of a bummer vacation had increased.

"Where are the mountains?" she asked. There were supposed to be mountains. The ad had described a little town out on the Edge with nearby mountains.

"Town's that way. It ain't far," he replied. "No mountains." He was lanky and dark, eyes hidden behind reflective lenses, voice laconic. There was something feral about his bony frame in his t-shirt and jeans. Like a coyote, she thought.

He looked her over skeptically and added, "The best hotel is the Rose. It's about halfway down the main street. Can't miss it."

He strolled off on some coyote business, leaving her in the heat and glare. "Thank you," she called after him. She was grateful for the snippet of advice. The Rose. That sounded nice. She had a destination now: find the Rose. Get settled. Maybe she would feel less disoriented once she had her nighttime accommodations sorted.

She headed out, plodding under the weight of the backpack. Lacking any signs or directions, she picked a path between two Quonset huts. On the far side she found a dirt road, and in the distance she could see the wooden roofs of the town.

She'd known this vacation would be rugged, but she was tough and independent and liked extremes. She'd been to the Arctic, to Mexico, and all over the US. She'd expected to find an odd little town, one that could provide experiences interesting and challenging but fundamentally safe. Now she had doubts about the safe part.

The little town lay baking in silence under the hot sun. She could see clear through, in one side of town and out the other, just by looking down the main street. There was no traffic light. The streets were rutted dirt. She couldn't see a single motorized vehicle parked along the measly, dirty, main drag. Some horses snoozed in front of a bar, a donkey wandered loose, and some chickens peckedand gossiped in a vacant lot. Other than the subdued voices of the chickens, the town waited in ominous silence.

There didn't seem to be many people out and about. A shop keeper emerged from the darkness of his store, glanced at her, and returned to his darkness, slamming the door behind him. The slam was over-loud in the quiet afternoon. A boy appeared, walking purposefully out of a side street, leading a pitbull. The boy had small, dull eyes embedded in a pasty, doughy face and lips that wriggled into a sneer when he saw her. The battle-scarred dog gave her a glance of stoic indifference. She knew they were on their way to a dog fight. Broad daylight—culturally normative behavior. This was not a place she wanted to be.

She stopped in the street to let the boy and his dog pass. Then, sauntering down the sidewalk as if they owned the town, she saw two tall dark men. They wore matching fedoras, their eyes were masked by shades, and their long dark dusters swept behind them like capes. She knew immediately that she needed to protect herself; she must not appear as prey to these men. She straightened her back, directed her gaze to the distance, and strode down the middle of the dusty street as if she, too, owned a piece of this town and had a right to be there.

She felt their eyes on the side of her face as they passed. They had noticed her. With an effort, she kept her chin up and her face blank. In spite of the acceleration of her heart, she slowed her walk; she knew she must appear unhurried. Behind the blank glass of shop windows, the locals watched her progress. They wouldn't help her if she was attacked. She didn't look for the Rose Hotel. Instead, she kept her eyes on the distant yellow line that divided the prairie from the sky. Back straight, chin up, eyes forward, she marched right straight through the town and out the other side.

She needed to find a place to hide overnight. Tomorrow she could catch a plane back home, but her immediate need was a hidey-hole, a place of safety in the blank, bare, shelterless landscape. Her only hope lay in distance and the falling darkness. She walked, still striding purposefully, swinging her arms as if she had somewhere to go, conscious that eyes were on her back.

Keep moving, she told herself, but don't run.

The hot sun of late afternoon cooled into evening and slid gently out of sight behind the horizon. Long blue shadows coalesced into a more generalized darkness. Then the air itself thickened to black as night fell. A fat silvery moon appeared in the sky, glaring balefully, casting a pewter spotlight on her as she trotted through the dark. Far behind her, the lights of the town were a low hanging row of yellow glitter. She stopped to reconnoiter. She felt vulnerable and exposed, even in the dark. Someone standing at the edge of town would be able to see her, even at that distance, even through the black air. She had to hurry, had to get farther away.

She strode onward through the night, stumbling occasionally on some stick or stubble. The moon subsided and stars appeared in the velvety black of the sky, but the air at ground level remained transparent, providing no protection. She was visible still, even from a distant viewer. She could feel the gaze of distant eyes. And then she heard a far off rumble. Some kind of motorized vehicles were coming her way.

Suddenly harsh lights appeared. Trucks were advancing toward her. Pickup trucks, their headlights bouncing, the engines growling. Five or six of them fanned out to herd her back toward town. There was nowhere to hide and she couldn't outrun them. She knew the trucks were driven by dirty, ugly men, and their intent was to rape her.

She couldn't do anything about it. She could only try to maintain her dignity, if such a thing was possible, by not screaming or crying too much. It was going to be horrible, nearly unbearable, to be touched by the hard-faced men with their jeering mouths, and she knew she was going to cry and sob and beg. The trucks closed in on her relentlessly. She stood still because there was no point to running.

And then she saw the cows.

A shuffling herd of longhorns, accompanied by the smell of dung and a fog of flies—grunting, sniffing, and snorting—emerged from the darkness, churning the dirt beneath their hooves. They were united, shoulder to shoulder, and their long smooth horns glowed gently like moonlight. Their kind brown eyes sought hers. She begged them with her mind, "Please help me."

To her surprise, the cows heard her.

The cows turned their attention to the approaching trucks. One by one the trucks braked to a halt amid flamboyant swirls of dirt. Engines roared and settled to idle, lights glared, doors slammed, and the hard-faced men jumped out of the cabs. They were grinning in anticipation until they saw the cows.

The cows, in a huddled dense mass, marched toward the men. They lowered their horns but made no snorts of threat; the lethal barricade of horn was enough. The men began to yell. Some waved their hats and some took a step or two toward the cows, but most retreated. When one climbed back into his pick up, the others followed suit. Doors slammed, engines gunned, and final insults were shouted. The trucks circled and roared off into the darkness.

"Come with us," the cows said. She was too grateful for their care to wonder why they were speaking English or to wonder how they could communicate silently into her head. She followed the cows as they ambled off into the night. She felt protected within the fog of dung and the cloud of flies. She traveled with the herd over a small rise that hid a pond from view of the town. Around the pond, the grass was deep and lush. The cows settled down to sleep, black heaps in the darkness. She curled up in the grass, not minding how dirty she felt. She was grateful to be alive and savored the sound of the cows breathing, their gentle snores and long snuffly exhalations. She lay in the dark for hours, her eyes wide open, listening to the cows sleep.

In the morning the cows were gone. She must have slept through their departure. She got up slowly and made an attempt to brush the dirt, cow dung, and grass from her clothes. She felt both stunned and oddly indifferent to her surroundings, no doubt due to the lack of caffeine in her system. Perhaps that was a good thing; reality was not to be fully faced this day. She needed to get back to the airport and catch that outbound plane with as little drama as possible.

Cautiously she climbed the low rise and looked toward the little town, barely visible as brown sticks on the horizon. The sky was a tender blue, the color of very early morning, and the air was cool. The fresh green grass of the prairie was decorated with tiny flowers. It was a subtly beautiful landscape marred only by the distant malignancy of the town. But no one would be awake there, she knew. They would all be sleeping off their binges of the night before. She aimed herself at the town and began to walk.

It didn't take long. And she was right; the streets were quiet. She walked down the middle of the main street, kicking up dust with each step, listening to the silence. She was about halfway through the town when she heard a low grunting sound. It was the boy with the pitbull. They saw her and stopped to stare.

The boy looked the same, a bit mussed from having been up all night, but still blank-eyed, thin-lipped, and sneering. The dog was battered and wounded. His lip was torn off on one side and one eye was swollen shut. She looked into the other eye and asked with her mind, "Why do you fight for that guy? If you're good at fighting, why not fight against him?"

The dog gazed back at her, thinking. The boy gave the leash an impatient yank and the dog turned, opened his mouth, and sank his teeth into the boy's leg. The boy screamed, windmilled his arms, staggered backwards, and fell. The dog let go of the leg and picked up his leash, which he then presented to her. She said, "You aren't mine. You belong to yourself, not him or me. But you can come with me, if you want."

The boy sat up. His expression was threatening, but he didn't speak. She wondered if he was cursing them in his mind. She turned away, hurrying toward the airport, but keeping to a fast walk so as not to trigger a prey drive in any local predators. The dog kept pace with her. He held his head up, on watch, ready to protect.

They arrived at the airport Quonset huts. She went from hut to hut until she found the office. The coyote man was there. Immediately she knew he could hear her thoughts, and that he knew she'd learned to communicate with animals. It was a frightening realization. She thought at him, "I'm going home no matter what, and this dog is going with me."

He answered, "Your choice."

She and the dog found a place in the shade to wait.

They waited most of the afternoon. She felt oddly calm, not entirely due to lack of caffeine. She knew, somehow, that she would catch the plane and would go home.

She woke up when something, maybe a spider, ran across her chin. The strange sensation rocketed her out of sleep, heart-pounding, startled and confused. It took a moment or two for her to orient herself. She was back in her own comfortable bed, beneath her voluminous comforter in the soft, warm darkness of her own bedroom.

"What a vivid dream!" she thought, as her heart climbed back into her chest and settled down. "I need to remember that story." Even the most intense dreams can slip away in the night, leaving nothing but a tantalizing touch behind, images which nag on the mind but are too blurred to interpret. To trap the dream in her head, she began to recite it to herself: the flight, the predators in the town, the rapists, the talking cows, the dog, the wait at the airport. She recalled her feelings at each point in the story starting with the initial confusion that curdled into fear, her determination as she passed through the town in the morning, and the odd calm while waiting for the return flight. What an amazingly detailed and clear narrative! But the spider that ran across her chin—was that part of the dream? Or was the spider real?

Suddenly she felt it again, multiple skittering feet making tracks across her neck and up her cheek. She screamed and slapped herself, flailing her hands against her face, neck, and hair. Then she erupted out of the bed, yelling, and flung the bedclothes aside.

"And there I was, sitting up in bed, my heart banging its fist against my ribs, and my mind full of the dream," Andrea told Coyote. "I didn't know if the spider was real or not, if it had run across my face once, twice or not at all. All I knew for sure was that I was finally really awake. I fumbled for the covers, pulled my blanket up to my chin, and waited for my heartbeat to get back to normal. And then I remembered how the dream ended."

It had ended with the woman deplaning somewhere outside

of town, maybe in a field. Andrea remembered how the story went:

She got off the plane with a vast feeling of relief, more than ready to plant her feet on familiar ground and wanting nothing more than to be back home, settled into her routines. Just to be polite, she nodded a farewell to the coyote man. He spoke into her mind and scared the hell out of her.

"Now that you have been to the Edge of things, we can always find you. Best to forget." He spoke casually, but the words shot through her like lightening. She backed away from him, stumbled into a turn, and fled at a fast walk toward town, the dog at her side. She thought to the dog, "You can come with me," but realized that he couldn't hear her. Now that they were back to reality, their mental communication was broken. He trotted off into the woods on his own.

"That's how the dream ended," Andrea said. "And I wasn't dreaming when I typed the story out twice, just to have the story sucked up into my computer. That really happened. So now I'm wondering, does my remembering of the dream mean that something really happened to me?" She turned to Coyote and demanded, "What do you think?"

As usual, Coyote wasn't much help. He just said, "I don't think so."

"The scary thing, the part that still kind of scares me, is when the coyote said that now that I know about the place on the Edge, *they* can always find me. Who are they?"

He frowned, thinking, finally taking Andrea seriously. "I'm

not the coyote in your dream," he said. "I think you got a glimpse into the afterdeath, but your mind twisted everything around because you were still alive."

"So no one is going to come after me because I remember that place?"

"No." Finally, Andrea thought, a definitive answer! "I think," he went on, "that you were dreaming about your life. You like animals and don't think much of people. Don't be scared." She checked his expression. As usual, he didn't look particularly concerned, just matter-of-fact. Then he added, "Maybe you'll meet some animal ghosts and you can keep them company.

7

Chapter Seven: Why is the Wastebasket Out in the Yard?

"Well, you know I love nature," Andrea said, "but there are some creatures that give me the creeps. Snakes, for example." She added earnestly, "I appreciate their role in the ecology and respect their right to exist, but I don't want them anywhere near me. I'm a NIMBY when it comes to snakes. And I can't abide a spider."

"Spider is an asshole, too," Coyote commented. "Not the same kind of asshole as Rabbit. Different kind."

Andrea waited, but he seemed to have finished his thought. "Well, anyway," she went on, "I was aghast when one caught me naked in the shower."

Coyote's black cowboy hat had vanished and instead he was wearing aviator shades that gave him the look of a preying mantis. Andrea blinked with surprise. He said, "Go on. Tell your story."

"Okay."

There I was happily sudsing my hair when this immense hairy monster started walking causally down the wall of the shower as if it owned the place. It was huge—at least three inches from toe to toe, and it had orange eyeballs on the end of its eyestalks. As I stared in horror, it *waggled its eyestalks at me.*

So of course, I jumped right out of the shower. What else could I do? Once I got myself to safety, I thought of the spider's peril. It might drowned! I turned the water off so the spider wouldn't be washed down the drain—though it probably wouldn't have fit, come to think of it. Still, drowning was a possibility, so the water went off. Then I hunted around for a way to pick the spider up without touching it.

The wastebasket! I grabbed it up and carefully pushed the rim under the spider. Obligingly, or perhaps in realization that it didn't belong in a shower, the spider hopped onto the rim of the wastebasket. I headed for the front door.

All would've been well except the spider didn't just sit in one place. No, it began to explore the rim of the wastebasket. As it sidled around toward my fingers, I started complicated maneuvers to keep a grip on the wastebasket while scurrying my fingers along the rim ahead of the spider. Thus the wastepaper basket was spinning faster and faster in my hands as I skittered down the stairs and across the living room to the front door.

I burst through the door just seconds before the spider reached my fingers. Desperately, I flung the wastebasket out over the yard. Then, before the neighbors had a chance to spot me, I ducked back inside.

Well, with my wet soapy hair, I had to finish my shower. And get dressed and so on. And it was my turn to cook dinner. What with one thing and another, I forgot about the spider until my husband came home. The first thing he said when he came in the door was, "Why is the wastebasket out in the front yard?"

8

Chapter Eight: Grandmother Stories

"Let's take a walk." Coyote got up and made his coffee pot and parfleche disappear somewhere into his old frock coat. Andrea wisped into the air and looked around. The sun was well up and radiating bright yellow heat over the gray expanse of sage brush and dust. The faraway mountains were grayed out into bleak vague shapes, silent and hot under the sun.

Andrea asked, "Are we in the real Nevada? Or some other place?"

"Real Nevada." Coyote set off strolling through the bushes. There was no trail. Andrea wasn't sure how he picked a route, or if he even had one.

"Where are we going?"

"Just somewhere else."

She floated a little faster to keep up. "What if someone sees us?"

"They usually don't see me. They might see you." Coyote gave her a glance. "But you just look like a shine on the air."

Andrea looked at herself. In the daylight she was nearly invisible. "Why don't people see you anymore? You said you used to talk to people."

"Sometimes I talk to people. If they need me. If they're looking for a message because they want some help."

"Oh." Andrea said dryly. "You mean you help by saying something obscure and they get confused."

There was a grin in Coyote's voice when he answered, "That's what tricksters do. Shake things up."

Andrea thought about his comment while they wandered through the desert. They were so far from any sign of human habitation that the rest of the America seemed to be a whole different reality. "The whole US is stuck," she said, "People saying and arguing the same old stale stuff. A lot of people could use getting shook up a bit, maybe."

"Well, there's too many for me to talk to."

A companionable silence fell between them. Andrea floated along, thinking about being shook up and open to change. She had been shaken up completely by becoming a ghost, but she was beginning to see some advantages. She knew the day was hot, but she wasn't feeling the heat herself. She didn't need to eat or drink and she wasn't tired. Did ghosts ever need to sleep? She'd been through a long night of loneliness and confusion, and now she was drifting aimlessly through a spare, dry landscape, the kind of landscape that could be boring or could allow wide range for the imagination. Yet she wasn't tired. She was...almost contented?

As she looked around, she noticed colors. Though superficially gray, the desert was composed of a palette of light tints of purple and blue for shadows, silver layers over bronze for the distant mountains, and fine mists of gold, lemon, and yellow for the grass. She could see a sheen of mint green in the small dry leaves of the scrubby bushes. The bushes were probably very old, she thought. Their stems were twisted and grooved, like ancient bent up old women. Between the shrubs, the sand was pinkish in places and in other places almost lavender. She was startled by the sight of a small white flower.

"Sego lily," Coyote said.

"It's lovely." Beauty in the small things. Is there a story in that? Beauty had a way of shaking a person up. Come to think of it, she'd spent a lot of her life looking for ways to get shaken up, sometimes by beauty and sometimes by something else.

"When I was a teenager we used to joke that someday we would tell our grandchildren about the things we did. We thought we were so rebellious, you know. Well, we were in a way. It was the sixties and seventies and a whole lot of shaking was going on. The war, the Civil Rights movement, all that. The whole US was getting shaken up. But we were middle class white kids living in a small college town in Iowa, so mostly our adventures were just getting stoned. Getting high." She shrugged.

"So you got any stories for your grandkids?"

"I don't have any. Grand kids, I mean. I guess I have some stories."

Every weekend we went out and got high. Pot mostly. I was never into anything else, but my brother was experimenting with alcohol. One night a bunch of us ended up in a restaurant with the munchies. I remember us sitting around a table talking, and my friend Debbie had a piece of apple pie. My friends all smoked cigarettes, but I didn't.

Here's a digression into a different story. The first time I smoked pot, I told my parents. They thought about it for a couple of days, and then they cornered me and said they wanted me to make them a promise. They said they didn't mind the pot, but they wanted me to promise that I wouldn't get pregnant, wouldn't smoke cigarettes, and wouldn't drop acid. I thought that was reasonable, so I made the promise and I kept it.

Back to my original story. My brother hadn't made any promises, and he did things that I didn't dare do. That night when we were in the restaurant, he was really drunk. So drunk that while we were chatting, he just casually stubbed out his cigarette in Debbie's pie. He didn't mean to ruin her pie. He just mistook it for an ashtray. We all thought that was really funny. Then all of a sudden my brother stood up and stuttered, "I have to—I have to go—I have to go!" and he ran out of the restaurant.

The restaurant was built on a hillside with a balcony on one side that overlooked a parking lot. We had parked in a different lot on the other side. Anyway, my brother ran out on the balcony, hit the railing with his stomach, and puked onto the parking lot. Then he staggered back into the restaurant in a total panic, yelling that we had to go, we had to leave, we had to run fast!

We were all so stoned that we just jumped up and ran with him, dodging around tables, and not thinking about why we were running. Once outside, we all scrambled into the car. It was a VW bug, so there was a reverse clown car incident while six or seven kids all tried to get into the car at the same time. We piled in on top of each other with my brother still frantically yelling to go, go, go, go! Debbie's boyfriend hit the gas and we went careening through the parking lot. We had to stop on the way out because a whole gang of bikers were muscling their way in. My brother ducked down on the floor.

It wasn't until the next day that he got coherent enough to explain that he had puked off the balcony onto one of the bikers.

Coyote grinned. "I'd run too if I puked on one of them guys."

Andrea laughed. "There are other puke stories about my brother. He came home late one night when my parents were either asleep or not home, I don't remember which. All I remember is he staggered into the house, crawled across the living room floor, and puked on the carpet. I ran over to help. He was moaning, 'Joy, joy, joy,' over and over which seemed weird to me since he didn't look happy. Actually he was calling for the dish soap, brand name 'Joy', to clean up the puke.

"One night, after he finally got home and in bed, his stomach boiled over and he ran to his bedroom window and puked out into the night air. It was winter. The next day, there was frozen puke all the way down the side of the house. Fortunately, his bedroom was in the back.

"I guess those aren't really stories to tell the grandkids." Andrea shrugged. "It was just being stupid." She hunted around in her memory and found a sunny afternoon in Iowa when she was fifteen. "But I have a little story about me."

For me high school wasn't really about having adventures. It as more like missed opportunities. I was so shy, I literally didn't make eye contact with people. I lived in my imagination, a classic case of a kid with imaginary friends. My imaginary friends were always in trouble doing exciting things, but I was a watcher, an eye. I floated through the day, watching other people and thinking.

I told myself stories all the time. While walking to school, while walking down the hall at school, while walking home, while swinging on the swing in the back yard, while laying in bed at night, I told myself full length serials, episode by episode. Funny thing is, I never once thought of writing the stories down. I didn't think of myself as a writer.

Every now and then I came up for air and looked around at the real world. I remember climbing out the window of my bedroom and sitting on the roof of the room we called the study. I was fourteen or fifteen, and I remember thinking about how someday I was going to die. My life would end. I tried to make myself really realize the fleetingness of life, the inevitable nature of death, the relentless passage of time.

I remember looking at the pattern on the sleeve of my cotton blouse and telling myself that I would never ever forget that moment in time, just sitting on the roof and looking at a spot on my sleeve. Every moment counts because none will be repeated and sooner or later you run out.

I couldn't imagine being old or dead, but I knew it would come, so I made myself a promise. I promised myself that at the end of my life I would not be disappointed in myself. I didn't know what I wanted to do with my life, but whatever I did, I wanted to not be disappointed.

"And I'm not, " she said, with some surprise, "Actually, I exceeded my expectations."

"That's a grandmother story," Coyote said. "You could tell your grandkids that if you had any."

"I guess you're right." Andrea laughed softly. "What I really wanted, when I was in high school, was to have adventures. And

I have had some. I rode a bike from Astoria, Oregon all the way to Quebec City, Canada. It took three months. We camped along the way." She checked Coyote's expression to see if he was impressed. He didn't seem to be. She tried a different story. "I stole a dog."

It was Coyote's turn to laugh. "What did you do that for? It's not like it's hard to get a dog, if you want one."

"I didn't want the dog. I just didn't want him to die of neglect." She cleared her throat and began the story.

9

Chapter Nine: I Stole a Dog

I turned off the engine and a dark silence fell around me. So far I wasn't scared about getting caught in crime. I was just a bit nervous about getting out of the car and into the solid black mystery of darkness.

I'd picked a starless, moonless night. Not on purpose. It just worked out that way. The air was thick with almost-rain, and the sky was heavy with clouds. Standing by my car on the edge of the pavement, I could see nothing. I might as well have had my eyes closed.

I flipped on my flashlight and immediately felt paranoid because there was a nearby house where people might be wondering who had parked on the road. No lights on, though. Probably a summer home and empty. Still, in the dark I was invisible, but with the flash on I could be seen easily.

I opened the door to the back seat and pulled my backpack out. It contained of all my criminal tools, carefully packed and checked at home. Nevertheless, I made myself take a few minutes to fumble through by flashlight, just making sure I hadn't forgotten anything essential. Then I beamed the light up the road and caught the gleam of metal on the row of mailboxes.

I set off. I felt excited in a way that was both gratifying and sickening. I loved sneaking around in the dark, but I felt sick with worry. This was not my first trip up the dirt road into the forest, but hopefully it would be the last.

The mailboxes marked the place where the little dirt road met the pavement. It was the borderline between the respectable world of water view properties and the denizens of the interior.

By crossing the borderline, by walking up the dirt road into the interior, I entered a world of shacks, rusting trailers, broken down trucks, and garbage; a world inhabited by people who barely survived from one Social Security payday to the next. Crazy people, amateur bomb factories, armed idiots who shot at Fed Ex delivery guys and other perceived threats, the chronically drunken, the chronically wasted, and the chronically stupid. Also cougars.

I strode out with determination up the dirt track, telling myself that the flashlight would scare off the big cats. And besides, didn't the cats hunt in the late evening and early morning? It was about five AM but still pitch dark. I walked on the grassy strip between the ruts to keep my feet from crunching on the gravel.

At the top of the hill, a strange dim glow to my right was the fence that bordered a strange compound of old bikers. They'd build their houses out of packing crates, recycled bits from older buildings, and scrap metal. Mostly they'd aged out of crime, though they were always high on something. During the day, I could see glimpses of their tiny community through the fence. They had a lot of trucks that no longer ran, had one Port-a-potty for shared use, and had a whole lot of cats. The fence was eight feet tall, painted yellow, and glowed weirdly in the dark. Above the fence, a square of bright yellow meant that someone was awake. I turned off my flashlight.

I was immediately plunged into disorientation. The darkness had lifted but not enough for me to be able to see much besides variations in black and gray with no sense of depth or distance. The fence seemed to be at arm's reach, but I knew it was more like twenty feet away. Trees loomed. I could sort of see the road but not really. I took a few cautious steps forward, and my feet snagged on underbrush. I turned the flash on and realized that I had started walking off the road.

I oriented myself once again to the grassy strip in between the ruts. Then I turned the flash off and, operating on blind faith, I moved carefully along, literally feeling my way by keeping my feet on the grass. When I stepped into the gravel, I knew I was getting off course and corrected. I had to make a conscious choice to not think about what I saw because the visuals made no sense; I couldn't tell if the black trunk of a tree was right in front of my face or six feet away. Carefully I negotiated my way up the dirt track.

By the time I reached the end of the compound's wall, having left the bright widow light behind me, the sky had lightened up enough that black had turned to dark gray. I could see the road as a strip of dark gray, though the trees on either side were still an amorphous mass of darkness. I picked up my pace.

The lighted windows I had been expecting came into view. The trailer was off to my left, slumped in the long grass and weeds of a clearing. Next to the dirt track, a dead truck was a big black lump. I could smell garbage and dog shit. I stopped at the truck and crouched down. I had arrived.

To get past the trailer, I had to sprint across about twenty feet of open ground in full view of the trailer windows The crazy old woman who lived in the trailer was always awake. I watched the window, and sure enough, her silhouette appeared. She didn't look out the window. She just stood silently and then stepped back into the filthy nightmare of her trailer interior. I'd seen the inside and I knew why the whole area smelled of rotten food and shit.

The darkness had receded a bit more. The trailer was settled into the weeds in a small clearing surrounded by alders and Douglas-fir. About twenty feet away from her front door, crouched against the forest, was a chicken coop. Between the trailer and the chicken coop, the grass was knee deep. I was too far away and it was still too dark to see if there was any life in the coop.

I gathered up my determination, made one last check of the trailer windows, and scurried across the clearing into the safety of the woods. There I turned my flashlight on again, and I started a slow examination of the edge of the road. I quickly found my candy bar wrapper. Then I turned the flash off again. So far, so good.

The candy bar wrapper marked the entry to my trail through the woods. I pushed my way through a huckleberry bush into the interior of the forest. The trees stood silent and dark, but I could see between them. Off to one side, I could see the harsh yellow glare from the trailer. The stink of garbage and shit made me feel angry and sad. I turned on the flash again but held it low so that the evil witch wouldn't see it if she happened to glance out the window. Then I made my way the short distance through the trees to the back of the chicken house. I'd sneaked through the trees so many times that I'd tramped down the little foresty plants and made an easy walk for myself. The evil witch cared for her dog so rarely that there was no trail through the grass from her door to the dog's prison.

She kept her dog locked up in the chicken house. The only reason the dog was still alive was because I'd been sneaking down in the dark for over a year to bring water and food. I had reported the situation to the local police who refused to act. I couldn't steal the dog and give it to a local rescue since the evil witch would find out. I couldn't just leave it to die of starvation or thirst, either, so I'd been stuck with the twice weekly task of feeding the dog secretly in the dark.

But this trip was different because I'd finally found a safe place for the dog to go. There was a mysterious collection of midnight rescuers who took dogs to an out-of-state rescue. A friend of a friend knew about them. It was an underground railroad for abused dogs. I just had to get the dog to my friend to give to her friend.

But I couldn't think about that. I couldn't think about *finally* saving the dog. I couldn't let myself get too hopeful or excited. In fact, I clamped down on my emotions and didn't allow myself to feel anything. I was there to perform a series of steps and I needed to stay focused on each step. So, with my breath regulated and my thoughts contained, I stepped though the hucks and into the matted down grass by the side of the chicken house. I heard a movement and suddenly the dog was there, his soft muzzle pushing against the chicken wire. He knew me.

"Hey," I whispered. Then I unpacked my back pack. I set my wire cutters down carefully by my feet where I wouldn't lose them in the dark, set the leash down next, and pulled out the fired chicken. The dog made a soft moan of anticipation. I picked up the wire cutters.

Then the sound of footsteps scared the absolute hell out of me.

I didn't even look at the trailer. I just went flat on the ground and lay there with my heart lurching around frantically in my chest. The heavy thump of steps stopped, started, and then stopped. Listening intently, I waited, frozen and stiff. The dog snuffled along the fence, wondering what I was doing and wanting food. Gradually my brain began to function. There had been no sound of a door opening, so the footsteps had to be inside the trailer. The witch was just walking around. She hadn't seen me.

I pulled myself together and slowly climbed up to my feet. Since it was still dark, I had to feel around to locate the wire cutters, leash, and chicken. The dog, a vague anxious shape behind the wire, was whimpering. He was a furry dog, like a woolly bear caterpillar. I knew this from having seen him in the daylight over a year ago. In the dimness of very early morning, I could only see the white fir around his nose.

I picked up the cutters. My hands shook. I had imagined this moment, the cutting of the wires, so many times that reality felt unreal. Don't get excited, I told myself. I took the first snip. My heart jumped. Don't get excited! Snip. My God, this is real! I'm really saving him! My fingers were jumping almost uncontrollably. Snip. Don't get excited! Snip. I cut a narrow opening and, before I was even finished, the dog shoved his way through and started inhaling the chicken. Quickly, I made a loop of the leash and lassoed him. Then I packed up the cutters, slung the pack on my back, and picked up the chicken. He gave me a sad look. It broke my heart that he was so defeated, so lacking in hope, that I could take the chicken away and he didn't even try to object.

I took three careful steps toward the trees, but I didn't pull on the leash. Instead I held out the chicken and whispered, "Come and get it." Scared but starving, he belly-crawled toward me.

I gave him some chicken and backed up until I was pushing against the huckleberries. Then I offered him another piece and once again he belly-crawled to get to get the treat. Then I stood up and gently pulled on the leash. "Come with me."

He yowled. My heart stopped. Morning had arrived and the protective darkness had receded into the forest. If the witch looked out her window, she would see us. I grabbed the leash right behind the dog's ears, gave a big yank, and suddenly he was through the hucks and into the woods. He took off at a trot toward the road, and I had to step quickly to keep up. When he got to the road, he stopped.

In the dim morning light, I could see him: filthy, matted fur and large dark brown eyes. He was panting, on the verge of panic. I tried to reassure him, but I was scared too, so I seized him by the lasso right behind his ears and set off with a firm stride. I more or less frogmarched him along. When we got to the clearing, I checked, saw no witch, and marched the dog ruthlessly to the safety of the woods on the far side of the clearing. Once on the road past the witch's property, I relaxed. The dog was still too nervous to eat, but he let me pat him and he came along more willingly. I walked him down to my car, put him in the back seat, and drove away.

"So that's a story I could tell the grandkids if I had any," Andrea said. "He got his happy ever after. The dog, I mean. He got a good home." This time, she didn't check Coyote's reaction to her story. Instead she thought about her own reaction. "I'm not brave at all. I was scared shitless of getting caught. I thought all kinds of paranoid things like what if the receipt fell out of the bag of chicken, and what if it had info on it that the police could use to tie me to the dog disappearing? Silly stuff like that." She laughed. "But I guess I can be stubborn when motivated."

10

Chapter Ten: Enemy God Kachinas

"Yeah," Coyote grinned toothily. "That's one for the grandkids." Andrea felt warmed by his approval. She tried to think of some other illicit adventure in her life, but was distracted by Coyote's odd behavior. He had his head up, his nose in the air, and he was sniffing the breeze.

"What's going on?" Andrea looked around. The desert appeared much the same as it had all morning. Perhaps the sagebrush was a bit more scattered and the lavender sand more apparent, but the mountains, gray under the burning sun, were just as far away as ever. Then she heard an odd creaking noise.

"What's that?"

A windmill under a cottonwood tree. An oasis. Had it been there all along, or did it just appear? The tree was full of the flutter of small birds, and the air was heavy with the sticky stink of fresh cow flops. Old and arthritic, the windmill was barely able to crank up water through its rusty pump.

Andrea floated over the sage brush to take a closer look.

The windmill creaked and moaned but water, precious water, spurted out of a rusted pipe into a tank. The tank was a little ecological zone of its own, complete with water plants and, to Andrea's surprise, fish.

"There's sunfish in here!" she exclaimed.

"We don't call them that here." Coyote strolled up and ashed his cigarette onto the dusty ground.

"Oh, maybe sunnies are a Midwestern fish and these are something else." The water was nearly choked with thick green ropes—some kind of plant what was too big to be algae but didn't look like any of the water plants Andrea remembered from the swampy lakes of Iowa. She watched the small fish flicker in and out of the green plant life. Dragonfly wings glittering in the sun over the water.

"I bet things are busy here at night," Andrea commented. She could see by the tracks in the dust around the tank that nocturnal animals came to drink. Some were cows, by the look of the cow patties everywhere.

"Stock pond," said Coyote. His eyes were on the distance, and he seemed to be listening for something. Andrea listened as well but heard only the sweet, soft whisper of a breeze. Then a grinding snarl from the windmill caught her attention. Angular and bony, it leaned over the tank like the exoskeleton of a giant locust-monster. Andrea had a sudden memory from way back in the nineteen seventies.

She and a friend had been wandering around the west, and they stopped at a trading post to do the tourist gawking thing. The store was packed with arts and crafts from the local Native community. Bold, elegant, hand-woven wool blankets hung on the walls. Glass display cases protected jewelry made of silver, turquoise, and coral. Andrea poked around, staring and admiring, but not buying. Everything cost more than she could afford, plus she had never been one to wear jewelry. Still, she'd been fascinated by the designs that evoked the patterns of the landscape: the layers of colored rocks, the purple shadows and pink sand, the contrast between dark green pinon and blue sky, the long flowing lines of the mountains silhouetted on the horizon. Andrea and her friend had been feeding their eyes with desert vistas for days as they wandered around the Navajo Nation and now, in the store, she saw those colors and patterns in jewelry and blankets.

Then she saw a display of dancing figures carved from wood and painted. Each figure had a card with a title: Clown Kachina, Bear Kachina, Mudhead Kachina. There was no explanation of the meaning of the dancers, just a brief statement that they were made by Hopi artists. And then her eye fell on one label. It said "Enemy God Kachina." The name lit her imagination. There must be lots of stories about that one, she thought, or maybe she could make up a story about enemy gods.

But she never did. They drove off across a landscape colored by the evening sun. Long blue and purple shadows lay across the red gold desert. To the west, mountains lit by the setting sun shone with blue light. To the east, the mountains had darkened to ultramarine. The whole desert was awash in color.

Drunk on beauty, they turned off the highway and headed up a dirt road toward Hovenweep. The primitive road, barely scraped into the desert, gave them an intimacy with the landscape; they were never sure their truck would be able to climb over the next rock or scramble out of the next arroyo. Every twenty feet of forward movement was a success. They kept moving because every turn in the road revealed another odd and beautiful rock formation.

Then, after grinding their way up a short steep grade, they came upon a flat open area occupied by a hunched monster. They stopped to stare. The monster ignored them. Its metal arms churned and its strange black head nodded, busily absorbed in the the repetitive stomp and lurch of its dance. The monster was frighteningly in-congruent with the landscape. And there wasn't just one. The sandy flats were spotted with them, each hunched over and grinding away at its own dance, ignoring the others. Andrea and her friend had driven into an oil field and were surrounded by the continuous, relentlessly drilling derricks.

They drove through the field of dancing monsters. On the other side, the road was smoothed and graded. They could drive faster on the easy road, but the sense of wonder and adventure was gone. They found a campground just before dark. That night, laying under the stars in her sleeping bag, the image of the Enemy God Kachina came back to Andrea. She didn't know what it meant to the Hopi artist who had made the dancing figure to sell. She only knew that she'd seen the enemy gods working away, drilling for oil, and they scared the hell out of her.

That was back before she'd learned about climate change. Her response to the oil derricks had been instinctive, visceral, not informed. After all, she'd been driving with her friend all over Utah and Arizona, burning dinosaurs the whole time and buying gas without a thought of harm to the climate. It was the following year, she remembered, around 1973 or 1974 that a biology professor told her class about fossil fuels and climate change. He'd warned her class that the destruction would be apocalyptic in about fifty years. Rising seas. Mass extinction of animals. Millions of people displaced. Disruption of agriculture and famine. Drought. Fire.

Now fifty years later, the enemy gods were still worshiped even while the world paid the price through mass death.

Andrea blinked and the vision of oil derricks vanished. She came back to herself, floating above a smelly cow pat in the soft dry air of the desert morning. The windmill groaned and moaned.

"Thank you for the water," Andrea told the windmill.

"No problem," said Coyote. He was still fixated on something in the distance. How could he take credit for the water when he didn't take responsibility for anything else? Irritated, Andrea turned away from the windmill. She, too, gazed out across the gray green sage toward the hot sunstruck distance.

"What's out there?" she asked.

11

Chapter Eleven: Not Much Reception

"Not sure," said Coyote.

"Helpful observation," Andrea commented.

Coyote shrugged. "You want absolutes? Or do you want the truth?"

"I was just being snarky," Andrea apologized, "but I can kind of see something out there. It almost looks like another ghost." Or heat rising from the sunburnt dirt of the desert floor. The sun was overhead and hot. Not that Andrea felt the heat, but she could see it in the wavering air. "Maybe it's just the heat."

"Let's go." Coyote strolled off into the brush. With a bit of regret, Andrea left the water behind. She kept her eyes on the distance silvery shapes in the air, wondering what they were— and realized that she wasn't afraid. She wasn't expecting the visions to turn into anything scary. I'm adapting, she told herself. Then she thought, I've never really had a vision.

"You know about vision quests, right?"

"Uh."

"I've never had a vision. All the time I've spent getting eyeball orgasms off how much I love nature, and I've never had a vision."

"There's more to nature than beauty."

"Oh, I know. Nature red in tooth and claw etc. Botflies." She paused for thought. "Guinea worms. The fact that most creatures are born to be eaten by some other creatures. I get that." She wafted along, enjoying the feeling of air moving below and around her. It was pleasant to travel by slow, low flight. "I did almost get a vision once, though."

During the nineties, after her husband's death, Andrea had gotten into the habit of going on solitary camping trips to the Rockies. Mostly she went to Glacier National Park. She had timed her visits to coincide with the flowers. When the subalpine meadows were in bloom, Glacier was Heaven. Trite, but true. If there was a Heaven, she believed, it wouldn't be all clouds and white robes. It would be lush mountainsides with pink monkeyflowers growing along the glacier runoff streams. It would be Indian paintbrush glowing in reds and oranges on the meadow edges, it would be fields of blue lupine and yellow blanket flower, and it would be bursts of white bear grass that looked like firecrackers frozen in time. Or columbine, as delicate and transitory as dragonflies. Glacier lilies, wild geranium, and the pasque flowers that bloomed in the snow. Andrea's heart swelled with the memory. "I'd like to see the mountain meadows again," she said.

I can remember getting up really early one morning in the dark. I got an early start because I wanted to go up the Going-to-the-Sun Highway before the traffic picked up. I timed things just right; I started the drive up the mountain in the light of dawn when the air smelled fresh and clean, and I had the whole road to myself.

The highway through the park crosses the Continental Divide by climbing up a mountain wall in a series of zigzags. The whole way up the road is a narrow trail between the mountainside going nearly straight up on one side and dropping down thousands and thousands of feet on the other side. There are waterfalls that spill out over the road. And flowers! Banks of them, hanging gardens of them. Red, rose, pink, pearly white, every shade of blue and purple, every shade of yellow. A ridiculously overabundant display of nature's creativity. Really, really distracting when you're driving.

Anyway I made it to the top without being so distracted that I ran over the cliff, and there at the top I was greeted by a committee meeting of mountain goats. They were standing around in the parking lot in a circle facing each other, very much as if planning the day's activities.

"Were they?" Andrea broke off her story for a question.

"Were they what?" Coyote was wandering along ahead of her. He didn't seem that interested in her story.

"When animals get together in groups as if they are communicating with each other, are they actually planning or discussing something? The goats looked *exactly* like a faculty meeting. Some even looked bored."

Coyote said, "Animals aren't like people, but some of them aren't all that different." He paused for thought, then added, "And people aren't as different from animals as they think they are."

They traveled in silence, Coyote loping along easily, Andrea drifting with her toes in the tops of the sagebrush. The faraway wavering shapes in the air stayed far away and waver-y. Andrea remembered that she hadn't finished her story.

Anyway, there weren't many cars in the parking lot. I drove in to take a picture of the goats. They all gave me identical looks of irritation. I didn't get out because goats have horns that are exactly at the right height to stab you in the femoral artery. That actually happened to a hiker. He died.

So, after interrupting the goats from their planning session—whatever they were planning—I hit the road and soared down the other side of the mountain. The west side is all swoop and swing, back and forth, as the road goes down to Lake St Mary. It's more forested on the west side, and the flowers are less distracting, but the wide view out over the valley made me feel almost like I could fly. Having seen lots of goats and masses of flowers, I was really in a good mood so I started singing. The words to an old abolitionist hymn seemed sort of appropriate:

My life flows on in endless song
Above earth's lamentations
I hear a real though far off hymn
That hails a new creation
Above the tempest and the strife
I hear the music ringing
Since God has love for all of life
How can I keep from singing?

And then I saw something on the road ahead of me. I slowed down and squinted. A hunched-over figure. Kokopeli the flute player? It sure looked like the image I knew from looking at petroglyphs. Stooped, rounded back, head lowered. I couldn't see a flute, though. I slowed to nearly a stop and stared hard.

Was I having a spiritual experience? A vision? I rolled a bit closer.

Oh. The hunched-over shape was a coyote taking a shit on the road. He glared at me, even more annoyed by my presence than the goats had been. Then he trotted off into the woods.

"So that's my vision," Andrea laughed.

"Yeah, that's nature for you," Coyote said. "From the sublime to the ridiculous."

"And I don't think I had the words to the song right either."

Coyote stopped and pulled a cellphone out of his pocket. Andrea stared, outraged. "You have a cell phone!"

He held it up and revolved slowly, "Yeah, but the reception's pretty weak here." He stuffed the phone back into his pocket. "I was going to google the words for you."

Andrea sucked in her breath and tried to figure out why the cell phone pissed her off. Maybe because it was too ordinary? Too mundane? She'd started thinking that her status as a ghost immunized her from the sturm und drang of life that played out in angry exchanges on the Internet.

"You google stuff?"

"Why not? I like to keep up. By the way, I got something you'll like." He pulled a battered copy of Science Everyday out of his pocket. "There's an article in here." He handed the magazine to Andrea but she didn't have the strength to hold it in her wispy fingers. Coyote deftly snatched the falling magazine from the air and said, "I''ll show you later. It'll be a bedtime story. I see some folks coming."

12

Chapter Twelve: Bedtime Story

The wavering silver air solidified into a trio of figures too disconcerting for Andrea's brain to process. They seemed to be composed of sticks and feathers, fur, old fashioned clothes, and random animal parts. One wore a top hat and the other two sported antlers. As she and Coyote approached, Andrea was able to identify the tall lanky one as female. Her long curved neck emerged from a bulky black coat and ended in a pointed bright-eyed face. At the sight of Andrea, she shuffled her black coat around her shoulders like a bird settling its wings. Her neck and face, Andrea noticed, were mottled and red, and her eyes held the expression of friendly skepticism that Andrea associated with schoolteachers. Miss Vulture, Andrea thought.

Next to her stood a short round man whose appearance was normal except for the antlers sprouting from his head and the beard which almost buried his small beady eyes. His barrel shape was tightly encased in a T-shirt that advertised the Tropicana. I'll bet he has *a lot* of back hair, Andrea thought. He must be a

Badger.

The third member of the trio barely looked human at all and had no gender indicators that Andrea could see. It peered at Andrea through huge, round, glassy eyes while rubbery lips moved silently. White fingers on blue-white hands waved rhythmically, and it s large ears flapped gently in the breeze.

Coyote tipped his hat and said, "This here's..." He turned toward Andrea. "What's your name?"

"Andrea," she said. The trio of weird individuals nodded greetings in their various ways. The woman Andrea thought of as "Miss Vulture" smiled pleasantly, tipped her top hat, and asked, "What are you up to today?"

"Not much," Coyote responded. "Walking around."

"I meant the ghost."

"Me?" Embarrassed, Andrea groped for an answer. "Uh... we're been telling stories."

Miss Vulture blinked her little black eyes and stared down her long nose. "Coyote tells lots of stories."

Her very dry and skeptical tone prompted Andrea into adding, "We've been talking about...spirituality. And time and nature and...related topics."

"All good topics for discussion," Miss Vulture agreed.

Badger interrupted impatiently, "Looking for a card game?"

"Sure," said Coyote.

They all settled down in a little clearing in the sage brush. To Andrea, the clearing didn't look natural—too round and just the right size for them all to gather in a circle. Coyote, Badger, and Miss Vulture seated themselves on handy rocks, but Andrea and the strangely fish-like entity hovered. Andrea noticed that it was barefoot, and its feet were dead white with long toes that undulated gently in the air.

"What'll it be?" Badger asked, deftly shuffling the cards from one hand to another.

"Five card draw," said Coyote. He grinned at Miss Vulture and added, "Did I ever tell you that story about how I faked Badger out when we were playing draw?"

"Nope," she said.

Badger glared. "You didn't fake me out ever. Ante up."

Coins dropped in the dirt. They hadn't dealt Andrea into the game, which suited her; she preferred to just watch. Beside her, the fish perused its cards carefully, pursed its full lips, and slobbered out, "Twee please."

"I had a pair," Coyote explained, ignoring the fish, "but I only asked for one card because I wanted to exude confidence."

"You exude bullshit," Badger grumbled.

"I''ll take one now," Coyote said. "I was exuding confidence because you, Badger, had asked for three cards, and that was a giveaway if I ever saw one."

"Twere's nothwing special about twat," said Fish, dropping its ante into the pot. "Every poker wand is a story about faking someone out."

They played five card stud for awhile, then switched to seven card and later Texas Hold'em. Play went on, interrupted sporadically by stories and minor arguments, until purple shadows lengthened and the sun, poised over the mountains, sent its last long slanted beams of light across the desert. Then Badger announced that he was hungry. Andrea watched, feeling left out, while the spirits produced picnic goods from their pockets. Miss Vulture even had a pink and white check table cloth which she spread out on the sand. Everyone munched their food and drank beer while they chatted continuously, telling little jokes and antidotes. After a awhile Andrea felt so forgotten that she checked herself to see if she was still visible. She was, but no one was looking at her.

Badger got up, stretched his back, and announced a need to go pee. Coyote, too, needed to drain off some beer. They headed in opposite directions out into the desert. Their absence created an awkward silence. Fish blinked slowly as if trying to think of something to say and Miss Vulture gazed out over the desert, her shoulders hunched. Finally Andrea broke the silence.

"You guys been friends for a long time?" she asked.

"Us?" Miss Vulture gave Fish a sideways look. "I've known Coyote and Badger for just about forever, but..."

"I'm new," said the fish. "Like you."

"I've only been here," Andrea stopped, amazed, "since last night. It seems liked so much longer! Years, even!"

"So why are you a gwost?" Fish asked.

"I don't know." Andrea shrugged. The lack of answers wasn't as frustrating or scary as it had been earlier.

"Usually it's unfinished business," said Miss Vulture. "Anything on your mind? Anything left undone?"

"Not really." Andrea thought about it. "Maybe...I came here to die under the stars because that's the closest thing I have to a religion. And all day I've been trying to ask questions about that. I mean trying to get answers."

Miss Vulture laughed and said, "Coyote hasn't been giving answers, has he?"

"Not really. Well, kind of sometimes."

"Beware," said Fish, "of anyone who says twey know twe answers."

"I kind of agree with that," said Miss Vulture. "Especially if you think of history. Just the same, life isn't a moral vacuum. And life is not meaningless." She peered down her long nose at

Andrea and added, "It's okay if some things are a mystery."

"Besides," said Fish, "twere is existence after deatw. Twere was existence before birtw too."

"You mean like...we're all made out of carbon molecules and so on?"

"Sure. It's true," said Miss Vulture. "Here come the boys."

With a crash, Badger shoved his way into the clearing. He flopped himself down on his rock with a big sigh. Coyote's return was quieter. His shrewd eyes went from face to face and he said, "Maybe its time for that bedtime story I was going to tell you."

Andrea looked up at the sky and saw that the stars were out. Her heart leapt with...not joy exactly. A glad but peaceful emotion. Gratitude? She tilted back her head, hurting her neck. Then she realized that, as a ghost, she could simply lay back on the air and look up in comfort. So she did.

Badger shoved himself back his feet with a groan. "Crap. We shoulda got some firewood while we were out pissing."

"Yeah," Coyote agreed, "We need a fire. I'll get some." He wandered off into the sage.

"I'll help," said Vulture.

"I don't think I can," Andrea said. She felt a bit guilty, but only a bit. The stars were seductively lovely, and she was comfortable on her back.

Fish said, "I can't eitwer." It fanned its webbed fingers. "I need gloves or sometwing."

"Do you like stars?" Andrea asked.

"Yes." Fish joined her in the air over the sagebrush. "I can see twe Milky Way."

"That's the Big Dipper and the North Star over there." Andrea pointed. "I love the stars because they give me a feeling of awe. Eternity. Humility. I can't really put it into words."

Fish rolled over so that it, too, was laying on its back. It said, "Seems to me twat...watever it is you're looking for it's sometwing you probably can't put into words."

Andrea thought for a while. "Coyote said that people understand things by telling stories. Stories are words."

"Sure." Fish flapped the long fingers of one hand. "We use words too. I just meant...if you catch sometwing into words, it's...'

"Less?" Andrea suggested.

"Yeah. You make it smaller, somewow."

The sound of spirits brushing their way through the sage interrupted their stargazing. Coyote was back first with an armload, followed by Badger who lugged a small log and Vulture with dry sticks for fire starter. The three knelt down together and got a small campfire started. Miss Vulture sat back with a sigh and said, "I love a campfire." Her eyes met Andrea's and she asked, "What do you think? Do you like campfires?"

Warmed by her attention, Andrea said that yes, she did. She added, "I like the night because I love the stars. I came here to see stars."

"Well, you scan see 'em," grunted Badger. He had a hot dog on the end of a stick.

"That bedtime story," Coyote said, "You ready to hear it?"

13

Chapter Thirteen: Let the Mystery Be

"I kind of think astrophysicists are our modern Druids," Coyote said thoughtfully. "It takes a lot of study to become one, the only people who understand what they're saying are the other astrophysicists, and their knowledge is arcane. They tell stories that no one else understands. I mean people hear bits and pieces. Like the Big Bang Theory. You sort of know what that is, right?"

"Sort of," Andrea agreed.

"Do you know what dark matter is?"

"Not really." She didn't really want to know. Her body felt soft and relaxed. There was nothing but air between her and the stars. Even though she was looking up at the stars, she felt like she was looking down, down, down into an infinity of space. The feeling was scary, but in a good way.

"That's the point," Coyote said. "No one does. The astrophysicists don't either, even though they talk about it all the time. It's hypothetical. There are gravitational effects that can't be explained which make scientists posit its existence. The story is that dark matter is abundant and is important for the structure and evolution of the universe. I'm sort of quoting here."

"Quoting what?" Miss Vulture asked.

"Wikipedia. But here's the thing. Think about this. Something hypothetical has a big influence on the evolution of the universe, but no one can see it or measure it or describe it except that it has effects which they can't explain any other way."

"Are you saying the astrophysicists found God?" Miss Vulture interrupted. "I totally disagree. Science and religion are not the same."

"Not saying they are. Science has a better track record, for one thing. I'm just saying that if you try to understand the Druids, you get pretty far out there into some seriously weird stuff. Makes you feel a bit of awe."

Awe, Andrea thought. I love feeling awe. Then she yawned profusely.

Miss Vulture smiled kindly and said, "Maybe you should lay down in your sleeping bag."

"If we're going to talk about stars," Coyote said, "we should all lay down."

Grunting and farting, Badger shook out a sleeping bag and flopped down on it. He struggled out of his boots and his T-shirt while Miss Vulture nestled down on her butt in the sand. To Andrea's mild surprise, she found herself laying on her back in the soft cotton of her old-fashioned sleeping bag. "How did that happen?" she whispered, but no one answered. She decided that she didn't care and snuggled into the bag's familiar warmth. Coyote remained seated, his yellow eyes aimed at the stars.

"So I read this story in Science Everyday," Coyote said. "The story is about a bunch of astrophysicists making discoveries about dark matter. To explain it to you all, I'd have to use their jargon and none of you are going to understand it anymore than I do. And besides, if I try to define anything, I'll just have to use more jargon and none of us will understand any of that either. So..." He shrugged. "So just roll with it, okay?"

"So I'll just have to take it on faith," Miss Vulture drawled.

"Faith that they aren't just making shit up," Coyote said.

"I know they aren't." Miss Vulture explained. "I was just being ironic. I have faith that they studied long and hard to become experts, and I didn't do that, so I respect what they say as informed. That kind of faith."

"Back to the story. Once upon a time, scientists were colliding particles in an underground bunker in Switzerland, and they got results that didn't fit with what they understood about physics. Something very strange was going on.

"They tried over and over, colliding their particles, and got the same strange results over and over. Every time they did their colliding thing, there were particles that weren't acting the way particles should act. There are four known forces of nature: gravity, the weak nuclear force, electromagnetic force, and the strong nuclear force."

"I don't like the talk about nuclear force," Andrea said, but distantly. Her eyes stayed on the stars. She was warm and comfortable.

"That's because it makes you think of bombs," Coyote said. "The forces in this story are the forces that hold matter together. Or make it blow apart. Or something. Never mind, just listen to the story."

"May the force be witw you," intoned Fish.

"I knew someone would say that. Anyway, so these particles in the underground bunker weren't acting according to the four forces. They were acting according to something else. 'Wow,' the scientists said, 'This is really exciting!' Some were probably seeing Nobel Prizes in the future. Another force! Would human minds be able to comprehend it?

"The force seemed to be inside the nuclei of atoms, down there with the quarks and electrons. Inside of you and me and everything else there are quarks, way down deep inside our atoms. Did you know that there are up and down quarks? And strange and charm and bottom and top quarks?"

"Strange quarks," Andrea whispered.

"Yeah, I like the strange and charm ones. Are quarks inside of dark matter too? That's my question but there's no druid here to ask. Anyway the story goes like this: Quarks decay and the scientists can measure them doing that. The weirdness is in the decay the scientists have been measuring. It hasn't been coming out the way it should, according to the four forces. So for five years they've been laboring over this problem, and now they are kind of tiptoeing up to the idea of a fifth force. They have tried and tried and nothing else seems to explain their results.

"Meanwhile, Japanese scientists weren't going leave all this science going on in Switzerland unchallenged, so they set up their competition and started decaying the hadrons with bottom quarks. No idea what a hadron is. And the US is in the competition, too, but coming from a different angle involving muons—-whatever those are. In the next decade or so, while the planet descends into climate change chaos—rising seas smashing houses all along the coasts, apocalyptic weather destroying the migration routes for birds—"

"Drought and heat forcing mass migration of humans and killing off the megafauna of Africa..." said Miss Vulture.

"The oceans craswing..." added Fish.

"Parts of the world becoming unlivable to man and beast..."

Miss Vulture said. "I mean places where people and animals used to live like around the Equator."

"Doom, deatw, and despair..." Fish intoned.

"Humans are weird," Badger commented.

"As I was saying," Coyote interrupted, "these scientists are expecting to reach the standard of test results to say whether there is a fifth force or not. It says that right here in this article."

"Well, the dead and the dying will be thrilled, I'm sure," said Miss Vulture.

"And this is a big deal because they think it might reveal dimensions beyond time and space. They think they might figure out what dark matter is too," Coyote finished with a bit of a flourish.

"It's a big old universe," Miss Vulture commented. "I'm not really faulting the druids for studying those decaying quarks or whatever while the world dies. It does raise a question, though, doesn't it?" Like Coyote, she tilted her head up and gazed at the stars. "I'm all I favor of learning for the sake of learning and knowledge for the sake of knowledge, but they're looking for the scientific answers to questions that no one can ever answer." She shrugged. "There will always be another anomaly, another strangeness, another hint of some possible force behind the ones we know about."

A vague thought drifted through Andrea's mind. Something someone said... "It's okay...with me," she whispered, "if it's a mystery."

Silence followed her words. A gentle breeze wafted the scent of sage into their camp. A branch popped and bright orange sparks shot skywards. Coyote watched the tiny orange dots drift upwards and disappear into the stars. The stars, he recalled, weren't necessarily there. Some of the starts had nova'd out of existence, but the light was still visible, traveling in their direction. He was looking across vast distances in time.

"Are you asleep yet, Andrea?" he asked.

"Almost," she whispered.

"Close your eyes. The stars will still be in the sky whether you can see them or not."

She did. He listened to her breath. Long breaths were followed by silences, then by light, gentle sighs. Her mouth hung open, and he could see a gleam of light on the saliva on her cheek. A silence lengthened.

"Is she gone?" Miss Vulture asked.

"Not yet."

Badger shifted his big body grumpily and muttered, "I'm not tired yet. Anyone wanna get the cards out again?"

"Too dark," said Miss Vulture. "Anyone have another story?"

Coyote said, "Andrea told me some stories."

He glanced at her silent form. Her body had relaxed as if her molecules were floating away from each other into small clouds of carbon, nitrogen, and hydrogen. A shooting star flamed out over the mountains.

"Gone now," Coyote said. "Anyway, she told me this story about going to Yukon Territory. Wanna hear it?"